Winter's Wallflower

The Wicked Winters Book Eight

By
Scarlett Scott

Winter's Wallflower
The Wicked Winters Book 8

All rights reserved.
Copyright © 2020 by Scarlett Scott
Published by Happily Ever After Books, LLC
Print Edition

ISBN: 979-8-696960-49-4

Edited by Grace Bradley
Cover Design by Wicked Smart Designs

This book or any portion thereof may not be reproduced or used in any manner whatsoever without the express written permission of the publisher except for the use of brief quotations in a book review.

The unauthorized reproduction or distribution of this copyrighted work is illegal. No part of this book may be scanned, uploaded, or distributed via the Internet or any other means, electronic or print, without the publisher's permission. Criminal copyright infringement, including infringement without monetary gain, is punishable by law.

This book is a work of fiction and any resemblance to persons, living or dead, or places, events, or locales, is purely coincidental. The characters are productions of the author's imagination and used fictitiously.

For more information, contact author Scarlett Scott.
www.scarlettscottauthor.com

He's the lord of London's underworld. She's the lady who deceived him. And now, there will be hell to pay...

Dominic Winter rules his empire with cutthroat determination, his heart as cold and dead as the January ground. Debts must be paid. Men must be loyal. Anyone who defies him will suffer the consequences, including the indolent aristocrats who frequent his establishments.

When a beauty boldly ventures into his lair and strikes a bargain with him to save an unworthy lord, Dom is captivated. Though his instincts tell him she cannot be trusted, soon, he will do anything to make her his. Until she disappears.

Desperate to save her beloved brother from ruin—or worse—at the hands of the despicable Mr. Winter, Lady Adele Saltisford offers herself in exchange. But one night of unexpected passion leaves her with dire consequences. Torn between her dangerous attraction to Dom and loyalty to her family, Adele flees London.

It doesn't take Dom long to discover the depth of her betrayal and give chase. This time, nothing and no one will stop him from claiming her. It's crime lord versus duke's daughter in a battle of the heart.

Dedication

For my readers, with much gratitude

PART I

Chapter One

❈

London, 1813

LADY ADELE SALTISFORD'S virtue was a small price to pay for her brother's life.

She reminded herself of the undeniable truth of this fact as she waited for London's most dangerous man to see her. Her hands shook beneath her silk taffeta cloak, and she was grateful once more she had not relinquished her outerwear to the hulking manservant who had ushered her to this anteroom. Her veil, too, was firmly in place, shielding her face.

Not that she expected to know anyone at a gaming hell dubiously called The Devil's Spawn to recognize her. Nevertheless, her brother had frequented this establishment. It stood to reason some of the society gentlemen who filled her dance card and flirted at musicales were also patrons. Difficult indeed to countenance, knowing what the fiend who owned it was capable of.

Maximilian had been badly beaten. Bloodied. The warning he had received had been dire. Mr. Dominic Winter did not care if Max was Marquess of Sundenbury, heir to the Duke of Linross. Max owed him an immense sum, and he intended to collect. One week was all he had left to repay. Adele was not meant to have discovered him as she had in his bachelor's rooms. But when Mama had fretted over his failure to appear at supper one evening, Adele had taken it upon herself to pay him a call the next morning.

What she had witnessed had broken her heart. But Max had been determined he would not seek out their father for assistance with his plight. He had sworn he would find a means of repaying Mr. Winter before the villain's paid ruffians revisited.

The man returned, his expression severe as ever. If murder had a face, Adele was certain this man's was it. He was terrifying, and yet, his countenance was handsome in an unexpected fashion that had quite startled her upon first sight. Now, she eyed his fists, massive as ham hocks, and wondered if he had been one of the scoundrels who had beaten Max.

He crooked a finger, beckoning her.

Whilst the man who had initially answered the door she had rapped upon had been only too quick to speak, mistaking her for a woman of ill repute and informing her she had the wrong entrance, the giant before her had yet to utter a word. She eyed him, heart pounding harder.

Misgiving blossomed.

She was sure she ought not to follow this wicked-looking man anywhere. What if he had no intention of taking her to Mr. Winter? What if he led her to a private room and ravished her?

He made a guttural noise and stalked toward her. Adele told herself to be brave, but when he raised his hand, she feared a blow was forthcoming. She shrank into the wall at her back, hitting her elbow on the plaster in the process.

His hand wrapped around her arm in a grip that was not nearly as punishing as she had feared.

"Unhand me, you rogue," she commanded.

But the manservant ignored her. Instead, he hauled her from the small room, pulling her into the hall with its gleaming wood floor and shocking, lewd paintings gracing the walls.

"Where are you taking me?" She attempted to wrest herself from the giant's grasp to no avail. "I demand to see Mr. Winter. If you dare to harm me, I shall have the magistrate upon you."

The man made another sound in his throat, part dismissal, part feral growl.

But he did not break his stride.

She felt rather like a mouse being carried off by a cat. This could not end well for her, in any instance. They reached a door at the end of the hall and the man paused at last, rapping thrice.

"Enter," called a deep, masculine voice.

It was him.

Adele knew, instinctively, who the voice belonged to. She had a heartbeat in which to prepare herself before the manservant opened the door and tugged her over the threshold as if she were the spoils of the day's hunt.

There stood her nemesis. Mr. Dominic Winter. His back was to her. All she noted was his coat—black, the cut fine, tailored to precision. If she did not know him for a heartless thief and murderer presiding over a vast empire of similar criminals, she could have mistaken him for a gentleman in any one of London's most exclusive drawing rooms.

Except Mr. Dominic Winter was no gentleman.

Not by birth, and certainly not by deed.

The thought of her brother's bloodied visage was enough to make her shoulders go back, her chin tilt up. Though she was the quietest of her siblings, she was not weak. She loved her family, and she would go to battle for any one of them. She could face this demon and save Max.

She had but seconds to summon every modicum of courage she possessed.

Mr. Winter turned. Slowly. As if he possessed all the time in the world. He moved with the innate grace of a large cat. With the predatory elegance of a lethal creature. But although she had imagined his countenance to be hideous—a reflection of his inner defections—she had not anticipated the reality of this man.

He stole her breath, and not just because his presence filled her with an ominous pang of fear. Rather, because of his appearance.

His dark gaze appeared almost black by the glow of the lamp. His hair was raven, his height immense, his chest broad, shoulders filling his coat. Even bathed in sinister shadow, she could see the plain truth of how wrong she had been. Mr. Dominic Winter was not a hideous beast of a man.

No, indeed. He was cruelly beautiful.

"That will be all, Devil," Mr. Winter said curtly, his voice a lash in the heavy silence which had fallen.

The brute who had unceremoniously lugged her into the chamber released her and disappeared with a surprising amount of stealth for a man his size. Fitting his name was Devil.

But the servant's departure seemed to suck all the air from the space. Adele was *alone* with Dominic Winter. Although she had done her utmost to prepare herself for this inevitable moment, her efforts seemed paltry as he skirted his desk and prowled toward her.

"Madam," he drawled, the lone word dripping with a combination of malice and carnality that had her pulse racing. "Your reason for intruding upon my day had better be worthwhile."

His accent was somehow lacking the unrefined edge she had expected. Either he had taught himself to ape his betters, or someone had seen to his education. Adele had imagined a ruffian who spoke with the lewd tongue of an East End pickpocket.

"Well?" he demanded when she hesitated in her response. "Have you a tongue?"

You can do this, Adele. You must do this.

For Max.

She swallowed. "Of course I do, Mr. Winter. The nature of my visit to you is personal."

"Personal," he repeated, sounding amused rather than irritated as he continued his approach.

Mayhap that was a boon. Not his proximity, but his tone.

"Someone beloved to me owes you a vast sum," she said, seizing hold of her flagging mettle. "It is my understanding that you are willing to accept an alternative form of recompense."

He stopped, leaving enough distance between them that a chaperone could not have found fault. And yet, she could not shake the sense his nearness was like a serpent, coiled and intent upon striking.

Awaiting the proper moment.

His lips quirked, but the chuckle he emitted held little mirth. "Who is this spineless cove, so intent upon saving his own hide that he sends a woman to barter herself rather than paying me what is due?"

Disdain dripped from his voice.

She stiffened. "He is hardly spineless. Nor am I his emissary. He has no knowledge of my visit to you today."

"Ah." The smile he gave her was feral. "The loving mistress, come to whore herself on her protector's behalf. How utterly heartwarming."

Adele did not correct his assumption. If he knew her true identity, she had no doubt this bargain she intended to strike with him would be even more disastrous. A man as callous and greedy as Dominic Winter would think nothing of using the knowledge to ruin her and bring shame upon her entire family.

If she had a prayer of continuing her deception, she needed him to assume she was her brother's lightskirt. There was no other choice.

She struggled to maintain her composure. To keep herself from thinking upon the result of her actions, should this man accept her terms. Her chest felt as if a weight had been laid upon it.

Adele sucked in one deep breath for daring. "It was my idea to aid him when he mentioned your amenity to debt cancellation with…matters of the flesh."

She had said it, though the words nearly choked her, and though the thought of submitting herself to this man's touch made her shudder and caused her stomach to twist into knots. Everything she knew of Dominic Winter made her find him despicable.

He laughed again. The sound held no levity; instead, it was ominous, sliding over her like rough silk. "If you have come here in the belief I will accept cunny for coin, you have wasted your time, madam. Devil will see you out."

With that pronouncement, he turned on his heel, giving her his back once more, and returned to his desk. The cut was an unimaginable slight. The notion of a duke's daughter being so ill-treated by a common criminal who had somehow swindled his way into the role he now occupied would have been laughable on any other day.

But not this one.

Adele was not amused.

Nor would she be dismissed.

Instead of meekly fleeing his lair, she followed in his

wake, desperation and the memory of her brother's badly beaten face making her bold.

❄

THE CHIT POSSESSED audacity.

Dom would give her that much.

However, if she truly believed he was going to bed her in exchange for her lover's duns, one thing she did not possess was the brains she had been born with. The Devil's Spawn could not be paid in quim. Therefore, neither could he. Not even if he wished it.

Dom damn well did not wish it. Except for her voice…

Curse her for having the voice of an angel. One could only suppose she had the face to match. Not that he could see aught behind her veil. Nor would he. She would be gone in less than a minute. Taking with her the delicate floral scent that was teasing his nose even now.

Lingering, much like she was.

He knew she was following him by the swish of her skirts. The sound of her every footfall nettled him. The minx was disobeying his edict. He had no doubt her protector was a soft-palmed lordling who had never needed to fight for his position in the world.

But Dom was not cut from silk.

He was torn from leather.

And he did not tolerate defiance.

He spun abruptly.

Too abruptly.

She had been in hasty pursuit. His quick action sent her slamming into his chest. The collision of her soft curves, coupled with the renewal of her haunting scent, made his pulse pound in a way he could not like.

His hands settled upon the sweet curves of her waist, keeping her from toppling to the floor. A jolt went through him at the contact.

"What the hell are you doing?" he demanded, irritated with her as much as he was himself for his unwanted reaction.

She was nothing more than a mistress who was deluded enough to heed the bidding of her cowardly lover. He did not believe her assertion the bastard had no inkling of where she had gone this evening or why.

Not for a bloody second.

"Forgive me my clumsiness," she said, her husky voice sounding embarrassed as her hands clutched at his shoulders.

Sodding hell, he liked the way she clung to him, the way she felt, pressed against him. Small and elegant and sleek. Not at all the sort of female to whom he was accustomed. He preferred his lovers to be from the same seedy rookery to which he had been born. Pampered aristocratic mistresses did not harden his cock in the slightest.

This one does.

Hades. The sudden snugness of his falls could not be denied. This would not do. She had to go.

"Why are you still here?" he snapped, setting her away from him as if she were fashioned of flame.

For Dom, she may as well have been. He did not deny his reputation had been earned in deed and depravity, but he refused to have it bandied about that he allowed stupid, selfish lords to pay what they owed him in petticoats. He had women aplenty willing to raise their skirts for him, and none of them charged thousands of pounds for the privilege. Indeed, they were only too eager to offer themselves to him *gratis*. Besides, he had far more pressing concerns that had nothing to do with seductive ladies in silken skirts and everything to do with greedy Suttons with iron grips on the water supply.

t efficient.

"Begging will do nothing for you, madam," he said over s shoulder, his tone grim, his decision made. "You may turn to your cowardly lover and tell him Dominic Winter ill not accept his Drury Lane vestal in exchange for funds wed."

Callous of him, mayhap. The finely dressed woman he'd had in his arms was an entire kingdom above a common doxy plying her wares. Dom may have been born to the rookeries, but he knew when something was expensive. When something was out of his reach.

"Please, Mr. Winter," she said, showing a fair amount of courage—or an actress's talent, more like—by clinging to her cause. "I will do anything you ask of me. Please do not send your men to beat him again. Or worse, to m-murder him."

Dom rounded his desk once more without ringing the pull and approached his uninvited guest. He was about to toss her over his shoulder when the last of her words pierced his cloud of irritation. He stopped.

"This protector of yours," he began, his mind working quickly, wondering at the odds, searching for a connection, "he was beaten?"

"Horribly." Her breath hitched on what he did not doubt was a sob. "By your men. I—I came upon him bloodied and bruised, his face swelled so badly I scarcely recognized him."

Floating hell.

"What is his name?"

"Sundenbury," she whispered. "The marquess. Please, sir. I beg you not to send more of your men…"

She sounded as if she were going to be ill.

Dom knew all the coves who attended his establishments by their vices and their debts, but he paid special attention to the marquess for his own reasons. Sundenbury liked gambling

"I will not go until you give me a chan[ce to persuade] you," she said boldly.

But there was a tremor in her voice which [be]denied, one that suggested she had never attemp[ted to introduce] herself to a black-hearted lord of London's underw[orld.] Pity for the troublesome baggage, he was Domin[ic Winter,] and he had sympathy for no one.

His lip curled. "You cannot persuade me, mad[am. Leave] before I require Devil to remove you."

Although her obscuring veil had made it impo[ssible to] view her face, Dom knew the sort of reaction the sile[nt giant] produced in others. Terror. And with good reason. Dev[il] had earned his sobriquet and reputation. That was one [of the] reasons Dom never allowed his half brother to stray far [from] his side. With certain East End powers at war, Dom ha[d to] watch his back for all the knives his enemies attempte[d to] plant in it.

"Will you not at least hear what I have to say before y[ou] refuse me?" she asked.

Curse her, but she was determined. And bold. And if sh[e] was as lovely as her voice beneath that damned veil...

"No," he told her. "You have nothing to say which would be of interest."

But still, the pugnacious creature would not go.

"Would you have me beg you?" The desperation creeping into her voice was not lost upon him.

He was not moved by it. Nor was he any more likely to allow her to say her piece. He had to ring for Devil before she started to weep. He turned and headed for the bell pull secreted behind his desk. There was nothing worse than a woebegone woman. Mayhap he needed to remove her bodily himself. Doing so would save time and irritation. Coldhearted bastard he may be, but never let it be said Dom Winter was and drink. Bad at the green baize. Excellent at draining the arrack and giving the bottle a black eye. Dom was in possession of a number of the marquess's vowels, and in the process of gaining more.

"Your protector lied if he told you my men were responsible for his basting." With that certain pronouncement, Dom settled his hands on her waist once more, the better to haul her over his shoulder and force her exit.

But damn it all, her curves molded against his hands in the most delightful way. What a terrible shame for a woman with a body so lush to be kept by a blackleg like Sundenbury.

"He would never lie about such a matter, not to me," she insisted, secure in her delusions. "I am begging you to spare his life and further harm. I will give you anything you want."

Her words should not have intrigued him. Should not have made his cock harden even more. Anything he wanted…

He had to face the stinging realization he very much wanted *her*. But not as the lightskirt of the Marquess of Sundenbury and not as a damned sacrificial lamb. Anger filled him, and he welcomed it. Rage was his old friend.

Rage was what he had built his kingdom upon. Along with cunning, his family, and his fists. And he was not about to put his power in jeopardy by allowing a luscious wench to cozen him into saving her lover. Especially not when her lover was Sundenbury.

"I do not want anything you have to give." He bent, wrapped his arm around her bottom, and threw her over his shoulder.

He was halfway to the exit before he realized the feisty woman who had intruded upon his day with her demands had yet to offer a word of resistance. Before he realized her body was draped over his like a lifeless sack, her arms bouncing listlessly off his back with each purposeful stride he took.

Devil approached him with a questioning look and an accompanying growl.

Dom sighed.

Either the troublesome female had swooned, or she was the greatest actress of the young century.

Chapter Two

❄

DO NOT MOVE. Do not blink. Do not twitch. Do nothing to make him realize you are awake. Everything depends on it, on you.

Adele berated herself as she was laid upon a piece of furniture—what felt like a bed, much to her horror. Although she had done her utmost to prepare herself for the sacrifice she would have to make for Max, being on a bed, alone with the demonic, beautiful man who had been so terrifying, made her heart pound and her mouth go dry.

Where had he taken her?

Whose bed was she on?

Surely it was not *his*?

Feigning a swoon had not, perhaps, been the best idea she had ever entertained. However, in the moment Dominic Winter had tossed her cavalierly over his shoulder, so intent upon being rid of her he was willing to extract her by force, it had been the only tactic which had risen to her befuddled mind.

Her veil and hat, which had remained happily in place for the duration of her impromptu upside-down travels, was removed. The pins keeping it sternly in place for the sake of her modesty plucked out some of her hair. Adele could not quell the hiss of her breath or the flutter of her eyelids at the unexpected action and accompanying twinge of pain.

Drat.

Her heart pounded.

She prayed he had not seen her reaction.

"You may as well open your eyes now, madam," came the low, gruff voice.

How she wished that voice did not settle over her like a caress, sinking low into her belly in a tangle of unwanted, confused sensations. This man was evil personified, she reminded herself. He was baseborn and greedy, violent and murderous.

Dangerous.

Untrustworthy.

Capable of anything. Responsible for Max's brutal beating although he denied it.

She kept her eyes closed and breathed carefully, attempting to remain as still as possible. She was not ready to face him yet. Not ready for him to attempt to send her out the door once more. It was not every night she could steal away from her family unnoticed. And it was not anything ordinary she was fighting to protect.

It was her beloved brother. His life, his welfare. She would do anything to help him. What other choice did she have?

"I saw you wince when I removed your hat and veil," he said.

Adele fought the urge to bite her lip. What was she to do now?

Think, Adele! Think!

The sudden weight of a large hand upon her breast shocked her out of inaction. Long fingers squeezed. Not hard enough to cause pain. Rather the opposite. Stunning, unexpected pleasure rippled through Adele. *Good heavens*, he was cupping her possessively, touching her in a place no man before him had ever dared. Her nipple hardened into a tight peak beneath her stays.

A diabolically handsome face hovered above hers. She blinked, falling into those obsidian eyes, noting the rakish manner in which a lock of midnight hair fell over his brow. How was it possible a heartless villain with such a black soul could be so staggeringly beautiful?

"As I thought," he pronounced, his tone forbidding.

His hand relinquished her breast.

She swallowed, trying not to mourn the loss of his touch. How foolish such a sensation would be. The product, she had no doubt, of her confusion. Mayhap even the result of being tossed over his monstrous shoulder. She was dizzy and terrified for her brother's life, and that was all.

"Where have you brought me?" she demanded, struggling to right herself.

He did not need to answer her query, for she could see where he had taken her. To a bedchamber. A surprisingly sumptuous one at that. The space was thoroughly masculine, and it smelled of him in a way she did not find at all disagreeable. Quite the opposite, in fact. Apparently, scoundrels could smell as inviting as the most perfect gentlemen.

Who knew?

"Do not play the coquette with me, madam," he told her sternly. "Though you have the face of an angel, we both know you are no stranger to the bedroom."

She tried not to allow his taunt to sting. Because she wanted him to believe she was Max's mistress. She *had* to make him believe it. Everything weighed upon her ability to make this terrifying man do what she wanted.

"Forgive me for swooning." Adele forced herself into a sitting position on the edge of the bed.

Good heavens, it seemed to have been fashioned for a

monster.

Which was just what Dominic Winter was, she reminded herself sternly.

He seated himself on the bed at her side, the dip in the mattress from his large body forcing her to plant her hands on the counterpane to keep from sliding against him.

"You must think me an imbecile," he said, his calm pronouncement quite taking her by surprise.

She thought him a great many things. But it was plain to see he was an intelligent man. Her heart pounded. Adele feared she was doomed regardless of her response.

"Of course I do not think that, Mr. Winter," she managed past the trepidation clogging her throat.

"Perhaps, then, you believe yourself such an incomparable beauty you thought I would be overwhelmed by the urge to bed you after I saw your face." His dark gaze assessing her as he spoke.

"No," she denied, a strange sensation unfurling at the way his eyes traveled over her.

Fear, surely.

His stare dipped, lingering on her lips. "I will admit, I am surprised a fool like Sundenbury could secure a woman as lovely as you. Did he promise you a pretty fortune for your favors?"

Max was not a fool.

A scapegrace, mayhap. Reckless and wild. In need of taming. But how dare this villain pay him insult? Adele clung to her outrage, chasing the other, unwanted feeling Mr. Winter provoked in her.

"My relationship with his lordship is none of your concern," she told him coolly, wishing she was not currently seated upon a bed. In dangerous proximity to this criminal.

"You are either as foolish as Sundenbury, or you have the

daring of ten men." He reached out then, trailing his forefinger along her jaw.

Adele forced herself to remain still. His touch was gentle. The pad of his finger was rough. Not unlike the contrast between hard and soft, darkness and light, right and wrong. She shivered, but not because she was cold.

The rasp of his skin over hers sent heat burning through her.

"I will give you anything you want in exchange for his safety," she forced herself to say.

His touch trailed down her throat next. "Anything?"

Adele forgot to breathe. "Anything."

❄

WHY HAD HE removed her veil?

Dom could have kicked himself in the arse for his miscalculation. He had intended to prove the lie of her actions. To startle her into wakefulness and be done with this game they played. Instead, the sight of her fragile beauty affected him. But still, she had kept on with her pretense of having swooned.

Touching the swell of her breast—that, too, had been tragically stupid. The act of a simpleton.

It had produced the desired effect in the cunning beauty before him. But it had also produced a decidedly unwanted effect in him. The same one which had been plaguing him ever since he had first touched her.

Now he was touching her again.

Her skin was creamy and smooth. Soft and warm and silken. Dom wondered if Sundenbury caressed her like this, if he had ever marveled over the texture of her skin or paid her homage as she deserved.

Then he cursed himself once more.

She had just told him she would give him anything in exchange for her lover's safety. Little did she know, the safety of the marquess would also work in his favor. If Dom had to wager a guess, the Suttons were behind the attack on Sundenbury.

But she didn't need to know that.

And he did not need to continue touching her.

Dom severed the contact, but the wild flit of her pulse racing beneath his fingertip haunted him, as did the sensation of her skin, burning like a brand. He rose to his full height, towering over her, gratified when she stiffened. Her dark eyes widened, the sooty fringe of lashes almost too long.

"Return to your protector," he snapped, irritated with himself for allowing her to prolong this pointless duel.

Irritated with her for wasting her loyalty upon a man like Sundenbury. Then again, perhaps it was not loyalty which motivated her but desire to maintain the roof over her head and the account with her *modiste*. Dom had not risen to his position of power by being a buffle-headed shite, and he knew enough about how women of her ilk worked.

The goddess occupying his bed feared him, as she ought. But she was also attracted to him. He had not missed the way her eyes had dropped to his mouth. He knew when a set of petticoats wanted him. And this one did.

"No." Her chin went up. "I will not go until I have what I came here for."

Again, she defied him.

Who the hell did she think she was, invading his territory, demanding he see her, pretending to faint, refusing to leave his bed as if it were where she belonged?

"And what is that, woman?" he growled the question. "What is it you came here for? Do you want me to toss up your skirts? I've already told you I will not accept a quick fuck in return for the coin that is owed me."

He meant that. Every damned word.

He did, however, have boundaries. He had not earned his fortune by beating the lordlings who patronized his establishments to death when they could not pay. Savagery was for Suttons. Winters were only bloodthirsty when the situation merited ruthlessness.

She paled, shock evident in her countenance. For a woman who earned her living on her back, she was remarkably quick to flush.

Still, she would not bend. "And I have told you that I will not go until you see reason."

Her temerity fascinated and repelled him at once. He did not think he had ever met another woman quite like this one. An instinctive urge within him told him to take what she offered. To take *her*. To kiss those pink lips which were surely as supple as they looked, to lower his body to hers, to lift the skirts of her gown.

But no.

He would not accept the leavings of a bloody marquess. Unless…

Suddenly, it occurred to Dom that discovering who had been behind her protector's bloody beating may actually help his cause. The Suttons and their dirty bargains and their infernal manipulations and their violence and greed could finally be overthrown.

No one would relish the prospect of Jasper Sutton getting what he deserved more than Dom. In fact, he would dearly like to serve justice to the arrogant son of a whore himself. And if the woman before him could aid in the quest, then why was he dawdling?

"If you truly want to save your lover," he said, the words

leaving him before he could contemplate the full wisdom of their utterance, "I have a bargain for you."

The lips he desperately wanted beneath his parted. "Of course I do. That is why I have come. What is it that you want, Mr. Winter?"

Mr. Winter. He liked the sound of his name in her throaty voice. Liked, too, the way she asked him what he wanted. The list was long. And depraved. Yes, he could use her in the way she wished to use him. A lovely woman beneath him, Jasper Sutton in the ground.

Paradise was about to dawn in the East End.

"You said you were willing to give me anything," he reminded her.

Anything.

Damnation, the mere thought, the lone bloody word, had his prick swelling and stiff once more. He had never bedded a fine lady; his bedmates were always women who, like him, had come from nothing. Women who had earned what they had, one way or another.

Much like the woman before him, except she was in a class all her own. Oh, she was not quality, to be sure, even if her silks looked fine and her beauty was enough to make a man willing to follow her to the fiery flames of perdition. Even if she rubbed feet with a lofty marquess, the mistress of a lord was not a lady, and nor would she ever be.

There he went, excusing what he was about to do. Offering himself forgiveness for his sins before he committed them. As the Winters did. He was his greedy sire's bastard son, was he not?

Dom's lip curled as he awaited his unexpected guest's response.

"Yes," she said at last, "I will give you anything in exchange for your promise Sundenbury will not suffer further violence. He is an honorable man, a gentleman. He will repay his debts."

He found himself jealous of her steadfast reassurances on her lover's behalf. First, the man did not deserve it. If he had been beaten by the Suttons, that meant he also owed them a small fortune, in addition to the tidy sum he owed Dom. Lord Sundenbury was making a fool of everyone around him, in the fashion only true gamblers did.

"I will send Sundenbury two of my men," he said, deciding upon his course as he spoke the words. More deliberation would have been preferable, but when had anything that had ever befallen him—from the state of his birth until this cursed moment—been preferable? "They will protect him from further attacks on his person."

A frown pulled at her lips. "But your men are responsible for what happened to him. Now you think to surround him with the same devils who did him such grievous bodily harm?"

Her shrewdness pleased him, and he could not say why. The inkling that this woman would make an enjoyable opponent could not be banished. Challenges had ever intrigued Dom. Baited him. Lured him.

He inclined his head, studying her. She was so damned beautiful, he ached just to look at her. Far beyond the loveliness of any woman he had ever seen. That such a woman had been ensnared in the Marquess of Sundenbury's net seemed the greatest shame.

"I am offering him protection, madam." *Damn it to hell*, he wished he had her name. "The promise he will not receive another beating. Will you accept it or not?"

"I will accept it," she said, without hesitation.

Sweet little lamb, all prepared for the slaughter. She had no notion of what she was committing herself to. If he possessed any compunction at all, Dom would feel horribly guilty for what he was about to do.

But he had been born without a soul.

Or if he had ever possessed one, it had been thieved from him as a lad. The rookeries tended to have that effect upon its inhabitants. Dom was no different. The wealthy Mr. Winter may have been his sire, but Dom had never been acknowledged. Nor had he ever been a part of the family. Disappointment was a taste he had learned at a young age.

"You have not even asked what will be required of you," he said slowly. Smoothly. Silkily.

How trusting she was. Either that, or she had broken the first rule of being a mistress and had fallen in love with her protector. She had reached the point where she was willing to do anything, to give whatever he asked, to save her lover.

An honorable tart.

Fancy that.

She eyed him warily. "I am prepared to do whatever I must."

How tempting.

Dom grinned. "Return here tomorrow evening."

He had to make certain of a few things before he proceeded.

"Tomorrow?" Her disappointment and confusion were evident, but her protest died a hasty death beneath the sound of rapping on the door. "But—"

One knock, then two in quick succession. It was Devil's signal that Dom's attention was needed elsewhere. *Fast.*

"Tomorrow," he repeated.

Chapter Three

❄

*A*DELE HAD MADE a ruinous error the day before.

And she was making another one now. She had always been the quiet one while her twin sister Evie talked too much. She was the wallflower while her older sister Hannah was the striking beauty. She was the practical one, the one who did everything right. Her brother Max was the softhearted ne'er-do-well, the charmer who perpetually found himself mired in one scrape after the next. Adele was the one who would never dare to flout propriety.

Until now.

She awaited Mr. Winter's presence in a surprisingly elegant sitting room—where she had been led by the same silent and sinisterly handsome man who had led her into Mr. Winter's lair the day before. Creating an excuse to avoid a musicale was one thing. Feigning an illness to avoid the much-anticipated Crompton ball was another. Thank heavens for Evie. Without her twin, Adele would never have been able to manage such subterfuge.

Still, there was no mistaking it—Adele had placed herself in a position most precarious. A lady's reputation was a silken thread, easily cut. If anyone were to discover what she had done, that she had been sneaking about London with the aid of Evie, hiring hacks, spending time alone with a coarse, baseborn scoundrel who made his coin by flouting the misfortune of others, her reputation would be irreparable.

What did he want from her?

Would he take her virtue?

How could she trust his word that he would aid Max?

The questions assailing her doubled and tripled with each passing minute.

Mayhap he would not arrive and his hulking, silent beast would return and escort her to the door as he had the previous evening, her innocence preserved for another day. Perhaps he would have mercy upon her...

She paced the sumptuous carpets in more determined strides when the door opened, stopping her. Those last two hopes died a swift death as Mr. Dominic Winter prowled into the room.

And just as it had yesterday, the full effect of his presence made an undeniable surge of awareness hit her. He was dressed to perfection once more, this time in all black, save for the snowy-white swath of his cravat. The knot was simple. The cut of his clothing fine, designed to enhance his masculine physique.

His glittering, brown gaze seemed to sear her as their stares tangled from across the chamber. Her heart thumped faster. Her stomach tightened. He seemed larger than he had the previous evening. More masculine, too.

The smile that pulled at his sensual lips was at once wolfish and pleased. He stopped halfway to her and executed a perfect bow. "And so the angel has returned to rescue the unworthy lord."

There was no mistaking the mockery dripping from his low baritone.

Adele dipped into a curtsy, ludicrous though it felt to stand on ceremony with this man. Yesterday, he had touched her intimately. In the manner of a lover, rather than a gentleman. A tingle swept through her at the memory. A delighted tingle, because she was a wretched creature.

How could she feel this untenable attraction for a man as vile as he?

She swallowed to chase the unsettling feelings. "I am not an angel, Mr. Winter."

Warily, she watched him close the distance between them. He rubbed the slashing angle of his jaw as he approached, and she took note of a marking on his hand she had not noticed the day before. It appeared to be an inking of a dagger, nestled between his thumb and forefinger. Adele had never seen anything like it.

"No." His smile faded, his gaze raking over her body in a stare that seemed to see through all her layers of armor, real and imagined. "I reckon you aren't, are you, love?"

His flippant familiarity made her flush as he reached her. She was hot from head to toe. "My presence here suggests the opposite."

"Mmm." He stopped before her, sucking all the air from her lungs. "I'm curious, angel. What makes you think you are worth my time, my attention?"

Excellent question. Although they could not be further apart in social standing, Adele had no doubt a man as dangerously handsome as Dominic Winter could have his choice of any lady in not just London, but all England.

"Intuition," she bluffed, finding her courage. "Regardless, I have come here to you, just as you asked."

He reached out, those long fingers catching her chin and tipping it up in a surprisingly gentle touch. "So I see. But have you come from your lover's bed this evening?"

Adele wondered if this was an ordinary conversation for a man of his ilk to entertain with the sort of woman he supposed her to be. She rather felt like a fish, plucked from the stream to flop about helplessly on land, gasping for breath. Everything about this moment, this man, was foreign. Frightening.

Potentially lethal.

For herself and for Max.

"Do not think of lying to me, madam," he said sternly when she hesitated with her response. "I can smell deceit in the air like smoke."

"I have not," she managed to say, and it was the truth. For she had no lover. She had only a brother who was beloved yet foolish. A brother she could not bear to see harmed again.

Mr. Winter was silent for what seemed a small eternity until finally, at last, he relented. "I will believe you an honest woman until you prove otherwise. And if you do prove otherwise…"

She shivered at the implication lacing his words. No matter how dazzlingly handsome the man before her was, and regardless of how her body reacted to his nearness and his touch, he was still her enemy. She must not forget.

"I am not lying to you, Mr. Winter." Her voice was surprisingly calm and unaffected when within, she was anything but.

His eyes searched hers with maddening effect. Her heart was thudding. Part of her wondered, quite foolishly, if he could hear its gallop. Nay, he could not.

Could he?

"Fair enough, angel," he said at last, a slight smile curving his lips. "You have come here this evening to make certain your protector is safe. I can vouch for his safety, provided you spend the evening with me tonight. However, I will not do the same for his duns. His debts remain. Do you agree?"

Here it was, before her with the finality of a hangman's noose.

Mr. Winter was promising no further physical harm would come to Max. And in return, all she needed to do was spend one night with him. She could do it. Of course she could, for the brother she loved so dearly.

Adele nodded. "I agree, sir."

"Dom." A flash of his teeth appeared as his lips parted on a smile that turned seductive. "No ceremony between us for the next few hours."

She was the daughter of a duke. She had been bred to respect propriety and her reputation, her adherence to society's dictates, as highly as she held the Lord Himself.

"Dom," she repeated.

One word, a truncated version of his Christian name. It ought not to feel so intimate. And yet, the air surrounding them seemed to change. To thicken.

He smiled, then. A true smile, the sort that made his dark eyes sparkle and fine lines feather from their corners. It meant he had smiled before. Many times.

She had pleased him.

And she liked it.

"Come, angel." He held out his hand to her.

His gloveless hand, the hand of a ruthless man, large and lethal, long-fingered. Yet elegant too. It startled her to realize how much she wanted to touch him.

She placed hers in his.

For the night, she would go where he led her.

And pray it would not land her deeper in the murk.

❄

DAMNATION, HER SKIN was softer than a lily once more. Her fingers, curled tentatively through his, burned him. Lured him. Tempted him. Dom was sure this entire affair was a bad halfpenny.

But there was something about this woman that made him willing to forego his instincts and to instead rely upon the all-consuming force propelling him to act. Lust? Stupidity? Arrogance?

Curse him to hell if he knew. Or if he cared.

There was something different about this woman.

Angel, as he had begun to think of her. It was not just that she was bang up to the mark, the finest set of petticoats which had ever been within his reach. She was…plummy. That's what she was. Only better than plummy.

Perfection.

Yes, a cove's word. And she belonged to a cove.

Not tonight, though. Tonight, she was *his*. All his.

And he was going to show her Dominic Winter's world. Or, at least, the best of it. Because there was quite a lot of it that was shite. No denying that.

He pulled her through the low-lit halls of his family's hell. The private halls occupied by his siblings, his servants, and his men. All the way to the dining room they had recently improved. A true sign he had reached heights he had never imagined possible as a bastard fighting for his life in the rookery.

Dom gently tugged her over the threshold, looking back to take in her expressive face as he did so. Her eyed widened. Mayhap she was impressed?

Her gaze settled upon a marble bust of some goddess whose name he had not bothered to learn. "What is this place?"

Could she not see the bloody table? The chairs? And a fine table too, commissioned instead of filched. Polished to shine.

"A dining room, angel," he told her. "We are going to have dinner."

"Dinner?" she repeated, as if it were a foreign word, a previously unimagined notion.

He stopped, their hands still linked because he was reluctant to end the tentative connection between them, it was true. She did not seem inclined to escape. Not that he had given her much choice. He banished the twinge of conscience accompanying that thought. He was Dominic Winter, *by God*. He took what he wanted. He owned this part of London. Even the goddamn rats knew his name.

"Sundenbury feeds you, no?" he asked her.

"Yes." She shook her head, her dark eyes meeting his. "Yes, of course. But is this not like fattening the Michaelmas goose?"

He could not stifle his wicked grin, nor quell the swift rush of his reaction. "Trust me, angel. You'll not be complaining if I eat you."

A slow flush crept over her cheekbones. Dom had not believed there were yet ladies in the world capable of being put to the blush. What a complex mix she was, exuding sensuality that was at once innocent and blazing. He rather fancied shocking her. Fortunately, he had hours to enjoy seeing how far he could push her. Of toying with her, in the manner of a cat with its prey, before he settled upon his feast.

Her.

"But that is the dessert course," he said, taking pity on her as he led her to the table. "First, we must dine."

She seated herself with the grace of any queen. There was something different about her, something that called to him. To the deepest part of him. And that was why he had struck this bargain with her. Why he was feeding her dinner rather than carrying her immediately to his bed.

Actually, that was not entirely true. Any ammunition he had against the Suttons was a boon to potentially aid his plans. And Dom was not the sort to rudely poke a woman. He seduced her first. He made her desperate. He brought her to her knees with desire, and he took her to the heights of pleasure.

He could not resist bending and dropping a kiss to the side of her exposed throat. *Christ*, she smelled like a garden in bloom, or at least how he imagined it would be scented, had he ever strolled through one. Fucking laughable, the very notion. Still, he inhaled deeply, savoring her. She was even softer here. Even smoother.

He had to fight the sudden urge to haul her to her feet, settle her upon his kingly dining table, and take her then and there. Instead, he dragged his lips to the place where her pounding pulse told him she was not as unaffected as she pretended though she remained motionless, her posture tense.

As a practiced mistress of a lord, she certainly had an odd way of seducing a man. But never mind. Dom rather enjoyed pursuit.

He brushed his lips over her skin. "Are you hungry, angel?"

"N-no," she said, stumbling on the word.

She refused to look at him.

"Do I frighten you?" After he posed the question, he licked the hollow behind her ear.

She shivered. "Of course not, Mr. Winter."

"Dom," he reminded her, rising to his full height and skirting the table to ring for the first course to be brought round. "And if I do not frighten you, then you are either brave or a fool."

He seated himself opposite her place setting, the better to watch.

"Perhaps I am both." Her serene voice, clipped in perfect accents that bespoke a genteel upbringing, slid over him in a serpentine caress.

His lips twitched, but he would not smile. Not yet. He admired this woman. Not many he knew would dare to challenge him in the bold manner she had. Desire unfurled.

"I tend to disbelieve you are a fool," he commented.

Her dark gaze clung to his, and he wished he could read the secrets hidden in her eyes. But the light was too low, and their solitude quickly interrupted by the arrival of his staff and the first course of the meal. Dom watched her take in the flurry of activity surrounding them. For once, he was pleased he had spent so much blunt on aping his so-called betters at the hell. His food, his cutlery, his plates, and his wine were as fine as that which was laid before any duke or earl.

The succulent aroma of meat and rich sauces hung heavily in the air. Dom found himself wishing he could still smell her. He licked his lips and found the lingering taste of her upon them. Would that it were a different taste altogether.

Later, he vowed, taking a sip of his wine to distract himself from his rigid cock, rising to rude prominence beneath the table. *Damn it*, when had he ever wanted a woman the way he longed for this one?

Never.

Fuck.

He drained his goblet and one of his efficient staff was at his elbow, replenishing his stores. Reminding him they were not alone.

"That will be all," he announced, which he had discovered was a fancy nib's way of telling the servants to remove themselves from the room.

His companion's eyes were upon him once more, brows raised in what he could only surmise was surprise. He waited until the door closed on the last member of his staff before speaking.

"Is something amiss, angel?"

She blinked. "Of course not. It is merely that I was not anticipating…" Her words trailed off and a charming flush stained her cheeks.

"You assumed I would carry you off to the bedchamber?" he guessed. "What sort of man would I be?"

She was solemn. "I have no notion of what sort of man you are."

No, he supposed she did not. And likely, it was for the best. He was not a kind man, nor was he gentle. Life had stolen all the softness from him. Dom could not seem to squelch the thought that this woman could bring it back. At least for a night.

"Nor do I," he told her. "Now do enjoy the meal. My chef is dedicated to his art. He is also a Frenchman. If our plates return to the kitchens laden with food, he will refuse to cook for an entire sennight."

His guest sent him a wan smile. "I would not wish for you to go hungry, sir."

He nodded. "Then eat, angel."

Chapter Four

❄

*D*INNER PASSED IN a blur.

Adele consumed enough from her plate at each course that her host's chef would not take umbrage. She still found the notion of the formidable Dominic Winter wishing to please his own chef quite entertaining. It was a detail she would pack away in her mind and revisit later.

Tonight, too many other things weighed upon her.

Last, but certainly not least, the impending loss of her innocence.

"Angel?"

Adele eyed the bare hand outstretched to her, absent of gloves, the fingertips worn with calluses. They were not the hands of a gentleman. She thought again of the inked marking she had spied on his flesh. His palms were broad and unblemished save for the common lines bisecting it.

She hesitated to place her hand in his, however. Indeed, part of her was prepared to flee into the night. To shy away from her every intention. But the reminder of her beloved brother's injuries returned, pointed and incapable of being ignored.

Along with it, this time, came the thought of this man's lips upon her skin, his tongue flicking out to taste her flesh. She shivered.

"Do you intend to live up to your bargain, or shall you sit

here all night, gazing into the ether?" he asked next, his tone cool.

If she had not known him better, she would say he was irritated.

But somehow, over their shared dinner, something had changed. Adele had witnessed a new side of him. A side that enabled her to believe Dominic Winter was not being an arrogant boor. Rather, he was afraid she had changed her mind.

She was a lady of her word. Regardless of the trepidation rising within her, she would keep her promise.

Adele settled her hand in his. "Of course I shall honor my word to you."

His fingers laced through hers, his countenance betraying nothing of what he felt. "Good. Come with me."

He did not ask or request. Dominic Winter was a man accustomed to giving orders and expecting those around him to follow. It was another unsettling observation. This evening, Adele was doing his bidding.

She had to.

But along with that knowledge came a shocking realization: she *wanted* to.

There was something thrilling about this man, this night, this place. All her life, she had tried to do what her mother and father had asked of her. She had learned skills she found uninteresting. She had donned dresses she deplored. She had done everything in her power to make them proud of her, to do them credit. Tonight, she was helping her brother, it was true. But if she were completely honest with herself, she would have to admit her actions were not entirely altruistic.

No, indeed.

She was here in this moment, allowing Dominic Winter—handsome, dangerous, undisputed king of London's underworld—to lead her to his chamber. And she was doing it because she wanted his touch. Because she longed for his kisses. He intrigued her. He also terrified her in equal measure.

In silence, they passed through darkened halls, then up a staircase. Until at last, they reached a closed door. Using a key he held in his left hand, he unlocked the portal, then tugged her over the threshold with their linked fingers.

And then, she realized where they were. In the same chamber where he had taken her the day before when she had swooned. A chamber with a bed. *His* bed.

Her entire body went hot, from head to toe.

Why did he have to be so handsome? She tugged free of his hold and wandered deeper into dangerous territory, seeking to put distance between herself and Dominic Winter and failing utterly.

Because he had followed her. Though he moved with surprising stealth for a man of his size, there was no mistaking his presence. She took in the pictures on his walls—turbulent watercolors and intricate engravings—before turning to find him near enough to touch. The heat from his big body radiated into hers.

He was staring at her in that bold fashion he possessed, the one which made her feel as if he could see her in a way no other man before him had. In a way that made her pulse pound and something deep within her quicken. Between her thighs, awareness throbbed to life.

She cleared her throat, reminding herself she was here for a reason. She had a debt to pay. A brother's safety to secure.

"What would you have me do?" she asked him at last, hoping he would not suspect the reason behind her question.

She was a novice, and not at all the dedicated, experienced mistress she pretended to be. What would a mistress do?

He trailed his forefinger over the bow of her lips in a touch that was so light, it may have never happened save for the sparks he left in his wake. "Seduce me."

Adele's pulse pounded. His finger had lingered at the corner of her mouth, so she acted on instinct, turning her head without breaking the connection of their gazes, and pressing a kiss to the roughened pad. His command filled her with a confused rush of longing.

He dragged his finger slowly over her lower lip and then slipped it inside her mouth. The invasion was unexpected and yet, somehow thrilling. She tasted the salt of his skin. Once more, impulse guided her as she sucked.

His gaze settled upon her mouth, darkening as he withdrew his finger, then slid it over her lips, moistening them. "What other tricks have you, love?"

Tricks? Angels in heaven.

She had none. She had never even kissed a gentleman. But she did not dare confess that. If he discovered she was not who she pretended to be, there was every possibility he would renege upon his word to keep Max from further harm. And Adele could not bear that.

Tentatively, she settled her hands upon Dominic Winter's shoulders. He was solid beneath her questing fingertips. Wonderfully solid. And male. And warm. She was *touching* him, this dangerous stranger who ruled over an empire of criminals. She ought to be terrified, but all she felt was intrigued instead.

"You are hesitant," he observed. "Do not be afraid. I shan't bite." He paused, sending her a wicked grin that made her feel as if her insides were melting. "Unless you wish it."

Bite her? The notion should have been repellent. And yet, issued in his deep, seductive voice, the words made heat slide through her.

What would a mistress do?

She would kiss him. Yes, that was what she would do. Adele licked her lips, imagining the proper way it ought to be done. Easy enough, yes? She would rise on her toes, press her mouth to his, and then…

She had no notion of what came next. Never mind that. She would figure it out.

Adele closed her eyes and blindly moved toward him, seeking his lips with hers. But his cupped hands framing her face stayed her progress. Her eyelids fluttered open to find him watching her.

"Eyes open, angel," he commanded softly. "I want you to see the man you are kissing. I do not want you to pretend I am another."

There was no one else she would rather have him be, though she dared not say so aloud. His dark, starkly handsome countenance stole her breath and made her heart pound wildly. He was everything she should fear and everything she had never dreamed she had wanted. The man before her bore no resemblance to the uninspiring dandies and lords who inhabited London's finest ballrooms and assembly rooms.

She rose on her toes, eyes fastened upon his mouth. Then, she pressed her lips to his.

And caught flame.

❄

SODDING HELL, HER mouth was so soft. So supple and warm. There was nothing particularly skilled in the way she kissed him. And maybe that was what made it so damned special. She kissed him as if she wanted to learn him. As if his were the first lips she had ever kissed. As if such unspoiled innocence existed.

It did not, neither in Dom nor in the beautiful woman in his arms. But something made him want to pretend it did, even if for the night. He wanted to pretend she was here with him because she wanted to be here, and not because she wanted to protect her lover.

Not so difficult to do with her lips moving over his. With each hesitant movement, she undid him more and more. Ever since she had first stormed into his private office, she had bewitched him. This moment was no different than all those which had preceded it.

Her kiss was almost tender. Sweeter than any kiss he had ever known. It was seductive and innocent all at once. Almost as if she did not know how to kiss. Her lips moved over his in whispers. She was good, this woman. Better than the other women he had known. Was this feeling why fancy coves kept ladies like her?

Dom had never understood the practice until now. He had simply taken his pleasure with women he could trust not to sink a blade between his ribs. He had never wanted another woman to the point that he would gladly give his left arm for more of her.

This one was different. He had not been wrong in his name for her. She was an angel. His angel.

For tonight only.

Unless he could manage to persuade her to give him one night more. And after that another. Then another…

Damn it all.

Dom had to rein himself in, keep the demons within him under control before they consumed him. She made a soft, whimpering sound. Almost kittenish. Her fingers curled around his neck, finding their way into his hair, which he knew he kept too long. Desire shot through him, sharp as a blade.

But he did not want to go too quickly. He wanted to savor this moment, this woman.

He was still holding her smooth cheeks, cupping her face, trapping her in the angle he wanted. Dom decided to take advantage. He deepened the kiss, his tongue sliding into her mouth. She tasted of the decadence of dessert. Luscious.

Her tongue moved against his. Again, it was not the bold invasion some of the women he had known preferred but rather a timid courting instead. There was no overt carnality in her response. There was only a delicious, measured surrender. As if she wanted him every bit as much as he wanted her yet did not dare show it.

Did she fancy herself better than him because she spoke like a lady and bedded a lord? Or was her hesitation part of her allure, a part of her elaborate act?

He had to know.

Dom sucked on her tongue.

She moaned, and there had never been a more beautiful sensation than this woman's fingers tightening in his hair and tugging. He had grown up in the deepest, darkest corners of the rookeries. He was a bastard, a man who had fought with his fists, his weapons, and his wits for everything he possessed. Roughness pleased him. There was comfort in pain. Almost as much as there was to be found in pleasure.

He nipped her lower lip, then soothed the sting with his tongue.

Her tongue chased his, sliding wetly into his mouth. There was nothing demure about her kiss now. She was claiming him, owning him, her lips moving with firmer pressure. *Good God*, had this been her plan all along? If so, she could happily seduce him whenever the bloody hell she pleased.

He would fuck her all night long.

Hades, what was she doing to him?

He was Dominic Winter. Ruthless, cold, and hard. He was never weak. Not for a woman. Not for any woman. And yet, this one, with her dark hair and eyes and her throaty sounds and her delicate kisses that turned into an all-consuming melding of mouths that demanded his complete and utter surrender...

Nay. That was all wrong. Dominic Winter was not the one who surrendered. Not even in matters of the fairer sex. He had to do better. To remember who he was and how he had fought to obtain the power he now possessed.

He was going to make her come. Again and again.

Dom broke the kiss and stared down at her, his heart pounding, his cock more rigid than he could recall it ever being. The pale-blue muslin of her gown, trimmed with golden embroidery, enhanced the undeniable beauty of her dark hair and eyes. He thought about taking her for the first time with her dress around her waist, because it was so fine. The fantasy of spending all over the expensive frock made his ballocks pulse and tighten.

But no, he decided. He would have her naked first. Mayhap he would even have her disrobe for him. *Aye.* A slow, thorough fucking. That was what he needed from this angel who had fallen into his devil's den.

"Your gown," he said, trailing his fingers over the embellishment that edged her decolletage. Her bubbies were perfect handfuls, her skin there so soft. And when he dragged his caress across her flesh, she shivered. "Take it off."

Her eyes were wide, almost innocent. He could believe, for a moment, she had never lived a life of sin. Those long, sooty lashes swept over her eyes.

"I require your assistance," she said softly, and then spun, presenting him with her back.

When had he ever spent the time to admire a woman's neck and shoulders?

Never.

Why not? He had to wonder now. Either this particular one had an exceptional back—would hardly be a surprise, that—or he had been missing a prime opportunity to admire a lady all this time.

He would make amends now, beginning with her.

His hands found her waist, and they molded to her curves as if they belonged. Nothing—not even a series of knocks from Devil that told him the Suttons were burning down the whole goddamn club—could keep him from setting his lips upon her nape. He bent his head and kissed her there.

Her skin was warm and smooth. He kissed a path to the place where her neck and shoulder met, then nibbled there while he found the tapes at the top of her gown and undid them. He kissed to her ear before catching the delicate shell in his teeth and tugging, then licked the rim.

"You...I..."

She was breathless. He liked that she was struggling to form a proper sentence, and he did not think it was because she feared him. Most of the people in his world—females included—were afraid of him. He had built his empire upon it. But for reasons he would not consider now, he did not want this woman to be anxious in his presence. Rather, he wanted her to know she was safe. That within these four walls, she would only know the height of pleasure.

"Me," he repeated, finding the second pair of tapes on her gown and undoing those as well before he pressed another kiss over her rapidly beating pulse. "You?"

He flicked his tongue over her skin.

She gasped, her head falling backward to rest upon his chest. Dom took this as surrender and nuzzled her silken cheek. A stinging rush of an emotion he refused to countenance rose within him like a tide.

Surely not tenderness.

Nor affection.

Nay. This was a woman he scarcely knew, and he was a man who took what he wanted without compunction. They had settled upon a bargain, and he was collecting his due.

That was all.

"I cannot remain here all evening," she told him. "We had best…proceed."

Not what he wanted to hear.

He dragged his lips from her throat. "Yes, you can. And you will. Our bargain is clear, angel. You are mine for the night."

And he intended to prove it to her.

Again and again.

He rubbed the coarseness of his whiskers over her throat, hoping to hell he would mark her flesh. That by morning, she would see the evidence all over her body of what she had done and who had brought her pleasure. That her protector would see it as well, whether or not the bastard had sanctioned this visit.

Hades. He would not think of Sundenbury now.

"Surely this—our bargain—will not require all evening," she protested, turning her head toward him, her gaze searching, as her body rested, compliant and so tempting, against his.

He smiled at her. "Sweet angel. Who do you think you have come to, begging for your protector's safety? I am not a cosseted lord. Everything you see around you, I have earned through blood and determination."

In other words, he wasn't a damned thing like the coves she was accustomed to. He was going to take what he wanted tonight, and she was going to give it to him. Not because he forced her into it—he had committed many sins in his life, but he would never bed a woman against her will. No, indeed. It would be because by the time he was through with her, she would be so desperate for him, she would be begging.

She would forget she had ever lain with a foppish lord.

He vowed it.

She stared at him now, her beautiful face a cipher. "I know who you are, Dominic Winter."

"You know my name, of course." His smile deepened into a grin. "How amusing you are, love. Everyone knows who I am."

Mayhap not *everyone*.

But the East End and a great deal of the West—the fancy coves like her protector—knew who he was as well. Because they gamed in his clubs, they drank his liquor, they fucked his lightskirts, and they were robbed by his street urchins. He owned everyone in this part of London. By design and by force.

He spun her around to face him then. *Floating hell*, she was pretty. Desirable. Delicate and ethereal and gorgeous and everything he could never have beyond the time he would have her this evening. *Sod it*, when had he ever been jealous of a cove? Never. Not once before now. He coveted this woman. He hated Sundenbury for having this precious gem as his own.

Dom had to have her mouth once more. He lowered his head and took it, this time controlling the meeting of their lips. He caressed up her spine, abandoning the loosened tapes at her waist, not stopping until he had her nape beneath his palm and his fingers sank into her coiffure. He tilted her head, angling her so he could deepen the kiss.

Her arms twined around his neck. Her soft breasts

crushed against his chest. She made a purring sound in her throat. He kissed her and kissed her, until they were both breathless. Until his lips tingled from the divine sensation of hers beneath his.

He knew then that he was going to do everything in his power to keep her. One night would never be enough. He did not give a goddamn how much it cost him, the ramifications for his plans. He would buy her fancy gowns and a fine house and worship her body every night.

All this pent-up need, all this soul-starving lust, and he had yet to remove her gown. He had not even seen the cream and pink of one bubby. Somehow, that did not matter. Nothing did matter but the angel turning to fire in his arms.

He told himself she was paid to drive men to distraction. That she was well-versed in the art of seduction. That nothing between them was real. Likely even the sweet sounds of her pleasure were feigned.

But they did not sound feigned. They sounded real. And they made his prick twitch. It was time to diminish the layers keeping him from what he wanted. He ended the kiss, cursing himself for his reaction to her. He was more breathless than a randy lad about to touch his first cunny.

He caught the delicate fabric of her skirts and began lifting. Hesitantly, she joined in, helping him to remove her gown. She stood before him in stays, a chemise, and a thin frill of petticoats.

Was his mouth watering?

He spun her about once more, working on the laces of her stays and petticoats. Never had he been more desperate to have a woman naked. He wanted to kiss and lick every bit of her gorgeous skin he could find. He wanted to suck on her pearl until she bucked and cried out and came all over his tongue.

Fabric dropped to the floor in a heap. He attacked the pins in her hair next, plucking until a sleek waterfall of mahogany curls cascaded down her back. Dom could not resist running his fingers gently through her sweetly scented tresses.

He released her with great reluctance, tamping down his steadily rising lust. "Turn."

Slowly, she did as he asked, until she faced him. The linen of her chemise was so thin, the pink circles on the peaks of her breasts and the shadow between her thighs were visible.

Floating, burning, sinking hell. Her nipples were hard.

"Take off your chemise," he ordered softly.

She swallowed, her eyes going wide. "Is that necessary?"

He would have laughed, was he not plagued by such mad longing. "More than air, angel. Will you do it, or shall I?"

Her pink tongue flicked over her lower lip, wetting it and leaving it glossy. "I will."

Damnation.

Having her remove her last undergarment before him would be delectable. "Excellent. I want you in nothing save your stockings, on your back in my bed."

A becoming tinge of pink colored her cheekbones as she grasped her chemise in her small, fine-boned hands. He had failed to notice how dainty they were previously, how perfect. They were not rough and reddened from work like most females of his acquaintance. The thought of those hands upon him, touching him, filled him with wild yearning.

He realized belatedly that she was flushing. Was her embarrassment an act as well, or was she new to being a mistress? Whatever the reason, Dom was entranced. He had never known a woman like her. Instinctively, he knew he never would.

She lifted the chemise over her head in the next moment,

and all coherent thought fled him. He drank in the sight of her—lush, womanly curves, wide hips, generous breasts…

He moved without realizing he was in control of his body. His hands spanned her waist. Her bare skin was warm and smooth, and it stoked the flames inside him higher. Dom scooped her into his arms and carried her to his bed, then lowered her to it.

Dom had never been so single-minded about the pursuit of something since he had come to power over the East End. He ignored his clothing—it could be shed later. He knelt on the bed, still fully dressed. Mayhap it was just as well. Surely he would shock her with his markings and his scars. Some women had been repulsed. Others had not given a damn after he had made them spend. This delicate siren, he had no doubt, who had only shared a bed with pampered lords, who blushed like a virgin, would be shocked.

Her thighs were clamped together. This would not do.

He caressed her calves. "Have none of your other lovers ever given you pleasure, angel?"

"No," she said, eyes wider still. "Yes. Yes, of course they have."

"You are lying," he charged without heat, for he did not mind. Somehow, the notion of being the first man to offer this incredible creature true pleasure filled his chest with pride and the rest of him with swelling, ridiculous need.

But she was not just lying.

She was also flustered.

And she wanted him. Dom was an expert at reading faces, at understanding what was churning through the thoughts of his opponent. It was how he had risen to the top of the rookeries, and it was why he had never lost a single game at the green baize. The scent of her desire was musky on the air. *Christ*, yes. If his mouth had not been watering for a taste of her before, it most assuredly was now.

He kissed a path up her left shin, to her knee, all the way to her garter, caressing her legs as he went. There was no denying the tension in her limbs, the stiffness in the way she held herself. Although he prided himself upon striking terror in the hearts of his enemies, the angel in his bed was the last person he wanted to fear him.

Dom kissed her knee, running his hands over the soft, supple flesh of her inner thighs. Above her stockings, her skin felt like paradise. He exerted slight pressure, parting her legs, and she offered no resistance. Her thighs opened. Inflamed, Dom kissed higher, discovering a mole on her inner thigh in the shape of a heart.

Fuck.

This woman.

He kissed the beauty mark, then nipped it with his teeth. She gasped. Her legs slid on the counterpane, and she was opened to him. At long last, he allowed himself to look at her fully, the dark thatch of curls on her mound, the slick pink of her slit, the swollen bud protruding from them beckoning to him.

"Yes."

The lone word, hissed, could have come from him. Could have come from her. He would never be certain. All he knew was that he could not exist for another second without having his mouth on her there, where she was wet and wanton and so ready for him.

That particular fact thrilled him most—he had scarcely touched her, kissed her, and she was glistening, the air perfumed with her desire. Dom's mouth latched on her pearl. He sucked. The taste of her—musk and spice and a note that was purely hers—flooded his tongue. He groaned against her folds, suckling harder, wanting more.

This time, there was no mistaking which one of them reacted. She moaned, her body bowing from the bed, thrusting into his face. He smiled against her, then ran his tongue down her seam to her entrance where she was wetter still. He sank his tongue inside her.

There was that same word again, burning through him.

Yes.

Nothing had ever tasted better.

Chapter Five

❊

*D*OMINIC WINTER WAS...
There was no word in her lexicon to describe what he was doing to her.

But his tongue. And his lips. *Good, sweet heavens.*

Bliss soared through Adele. Whatever it was that he was doing, she did not need words. All she knew was it felt better than anything she had ever experienced in her life.

Likely, it was wrong, too.

And wicked.

Shameful.

She would worry about all that later. So, too, the implications of what she was doing. Because in this moment, no other thoughts existed save him. He was everything she had ever imagined, ever wanted, ever longed for without knowing it, bringing her to life, making her burn.

His tongue, warm and wet and knowing, slipped inside her. She gasped. Never had she imagined such pleasures were possible. It was... He was... That wicked mouth of his had returned to the other part of her that was most sensitive. The part she had only dared touch in the privacy and darkness of her chamber. But the things he was doing to her—her fingers could never compare.

"Oh," she moaned as his teeth nipped her there. Not hard enough to cause pain. But delightfully. Wickedly. Her hips pumped toward him. "Dom, please..."

She closed her eyes and tipped her head back, trying to blot out any lingering pieces of her conscience. There was no room for guilt in this moment. She was doing this to protect her brother, she reminded herself. This was the cost. The price she had agreed to pay.

Never mind that Dominic Winter's mouth upon her flesh felt nothing like a cost or a price, but rather like a reward. She would fret about that later. For now, there was only sensation.

Incredible, all-consuming, decadent sensation.

Everything inside her tightened into a knot. His tongue flicked, and then he sucked again. She fell apart. Sparks shot across her eyelids and bliss washed over her entire body as she quaked beneath his sensual onslaught. It felt so good, too good. Better than anything she had ever accomplished on her own.

Of course it did, she told herself sternly. *Dominic Winter is the devil incarnate.*

He did not feel devilish at the moment, however. No, indeed. All he felt was...

Heavenly.

But he was not finished working his magic upon her, because he was kissing her again, moving up her body, raining fire everywhere he went. Over her belly, to her breasts. He stopped there, licking a tantalizing circle around her nipple before sucking it into his mouth. The part of her that was still pulsing experienced a new surge of yearning.

Her fingers threaded through his thick, dark hair. Touching him was an exquisite freedom. Lying with him in his bed was a dream. He blew on her nipple, the stream of hot air making her arch her back, seeking more. More Dominic Winter.

He made a low sound of appreciation in his throat, carnal

and raw, almost a growl. Then he laved the peak of her other breast with the same sweet torture. He was still fully dressed, and the slide of his breeches against her most intimate, sensitive parts sent a bolt of desire shooting straight through Adele. It felt so good, she could not resist moving, grinding herself against the intrusion of his thick, muscled thigh.

"Patience, angel," he murmured, grinning roguishly up at her.

The contrast between the pale curve of her breast and his dark good looks was not lost upon her. How strange it was that this man she scarcely knew, this wicked lord of the criminal underworld, could feel so right. The weight of his body pinning her to the bed, the tenderness of his touches, the pleasure he gave her…it was all at odds with everything she had expected.

She *wanted* him.

What was wrong with her? This was the man who had sent his minions to hurt her brother because of the debts he owed, was he not?

"Stop thinking," he said, his gaze seeming to reach inside her, searing her. "Stay here with me. Let me pleasure you, show you what you have been missing."

He dropped a series of hot kisses on her breast, all the way to her collarbone. There was more to show her? Impossible.

But he proved just how possible it was as he dragged his lips and the coarseness of his whiskers along her throat. As his body insinuated itself fully between her thighs. The thick ridge of him was undeniable, pressing into her throbbing center. All the breath fled her as he took her lips in a kiss that was passionate and bold and claiming.

She tasted herself on his lips when she opened for him. Their tongues moved together. His fingers slipped between them, and when his callused forefinger slid over the sensitized bud between her legs, she moaned into his kiss, hips jerking. It seemed impossible she could feel more. He tortured her with slow, steady caresses, swirling, bringing her to the edge before withdrawing.

Then he kissed along her jaw, all the way to her ear, his lips nuzzling her as he spoke. "Not yet, angel. I want you to come when I am inside you next."

His words should have shocked her. No one had ever spoken so coarsely in her presence. And yet, they made her want him more.

He nipped her earlobe. "You are so wet and ready for me."

He took her mouth again in a passionate kiss, and then the absence of his fingers was replaced by something else. The thick length of him brushed her folds, the slick sound of their bodies moving together making more desire pool between her thighs. He worked himself up and down, then over her pulsing bud again and again. The things he was doing to her…

Sinful.

Wrong.

Wondrous.

Nothing could have prepared her for this. For him. Dominic Winter was unlike any man she had ever known. Unlike any she would ever know again. Adele clutched his powerful body to hers, kissing him back with all the reckless abandon in her soul.

❄

DOM HAD TO be inside her.

Now.

There was no time to rid himself of his breeches. Licking

her had left him in a state of near madness. Saved him the trouble of fretting over his inking and scars. But he could not deny the desire to have her bare skin pressed to his.

Later, he promised himself as he teased her pearl with his cockhead. He would have her again this night. And again. He would make love to her slowly, savoring the sensation. If he had his way, she would stay where she was and he would spend the foreseeable future bedding her as often as possible.

But first, he had to be certain. It was not his way to bargain with a woman to get her beneath him. He did not think he misread her body's signals—she was dripping and the breathy moans and undulations of her hips did not lie. Still, though he had been born a bastard and a criminal, he had a sense of honor when it came to his women.

He broke the kiss, staring down at her. "You want me, angel?"

Say yes.

Please, God.

She must have heard his silent prayer—or some other deity did—because her swollen lips parted. "Yes."

Thank Christ.

He kissed her again as he dragged his cock along her slit, finding her entrance. No greater temptation existed than the promise of her cunny. His tongue slid past her lips as he slowly sank inside her. Tight heat bathed him.

Heaven right here in the East End.

She felt so good, wrapped around his aching cock, constricting on him with almost painful pleasure. He held himself still, then moved. There was a moment of resistance, almost as if her body was reluctant to accept his despite her readiness for him. He fed her more kisses and stroked her pearl until her hips were moving again, her body undulating beneath his, dragging him deeper inside her.

Nothing could stop him from basking in the divine sensation of her stretched around him, her pliant, lush curves supple beneath his body. If an entire army of Suttons had come rushing into his private apartments just then, he would not have stopped making love to this woman.

What power did she have over him?

He would worry about that later, when he was not buried inside her sweet cunny. For now, all he could do was take them to the inevitable conclusion. He wanted her to spend on his cock.

Everything in him throbbed with the urge for more. To move. And so he did, relinquishing her mouth to suck on her nipples as he thrust in and out of her hot cunny. She moaned, the low sound spurring him on.

And on.

He was so lost in her that when she reached her pinnacle, clenching on him and tremoring all around his cock in decadent quivers, he was unprepared. On a cry, he surged deeper, his own spend rushing from him before he could withdraw. White-hot pleasure ran through him as he emptied inside her, her tight walls milking him of everything he had.

He sealed their lips in another slow, maddening kiss, and then he rolled to his side, still fully dressed save for his bare cock, which glistened with a combination of her dew and his mettle. He had just experienced the single most glorious moment of his existence. But he had made a stupid, careless mistake.

Fucking hell.

Dom knew better. He had spent his life in the shadows, the bastard son of a man who reviled him and his mother both. Never would he wish to foist the same curse upon any spawn of his own. Indeed, he had done his utmost thus far to make certain there was nary a possibility of it.

What was his excuse?

How had he lost his legendary control so desperately?

She had felt so good. Too good. Tight and warm and wet. That had been part of the problem. But the other part was simply *her*. There was something about this woman. Something that burrowed deep inside him, dwelling within a place he had not known existed.

A place that bloody well ought to have been turned to ash like all the rest of him.

"Forgive me," he told her. "I should have possessed more restraint."

Her hair was a dark halo about her lovely face. She looked flushed and sated, and the mere sight of her made him want to make love to her again. He was going to keep her here. There was no doubt. This woman was *his*, and when Dominic Winter saw something he wanted, he seized it.

"You need not apologize," she told him softly—demurely. "I...enjoyed it very much."

Floating hell, this divine creature who had somehow fallen into his gaming hell like a gift from above. What would he do with her?

Everything.

That was what he would do with her. And then he would do it again.

But first, he needed to tend to her. He rose from the bed, straightening and fastening the fall of his breeches. Then he gathered cloth, bowl, and water. When he returned, she was where he had left her, sound asleep.

A profound rush of tenderness hit him in the chest.

Then, Dominic Winter did something he had never done before.

He tucked a counterpane around his soundly sleeping lover, and he joined her on the bed, molding his body to hers. Within moments, he, too, was falling headlong into the welcoming abyss of slumber.

PART II

Chapter Six

Oxfordshire
Two months later

THE DAY WAS colder than a whore's heart.

Only a Bedlamite would have dared to travel from London on nigh impassable, snow-covered roads to the country in the midst of the most frigid winter in memory. But Dominic Winter was not mad. No, indeed.

He was instead, he thought with a nasty smile as his carriage laboriously plodded over the icy country lanes, a man with an overzealous need. Because two months ago, he had been visited in London by an angel.

And then, she had disappeared.

Devil had warned Dom he was making a grievous error in accepting the bargain with Sundenbury's lightskirt. But Dom was oldest, and he never listened when any of his miscellany of half siblings bothered to warn him from the path he had chosen. He was the leader of this family, *by Hades*, and he would lead it as he saw fit.

This time, however, Devil had been right.

Not that Devil was ever wrong. A man of few words, his brother used them to advantage when he actually deigned to employ them. Which was why Dom kept Devil close, as his right-hand man. He was far more reliable than Gavin, who cared more for his prizefighting than he did for the business end of their familial dealings. Far less deadly than Blade, whose skills were put to better uses—namely, dispatching enemies. More practical than Demon, who preferred to spend his time charming ladies and playing the game. And Genevieve? Well, their wily sister was too busy attempting to run her own rookery empire.

What Devil could not have known, and what Dom himself had only finally, at long last, discovered, was that his angel was not at all what he had presumed her to be. Far from being the mistress of a fancy cove, she was the daughter of an even fancier one. A duke's daughter, to be precise.

"Lady Adele Saltisford," he said aloud into the creak-interrupted silence of his carriage, trying her name on his tongue.

Pity that by the time he had realized the woman who had become his unfortunate obsession—the one he had torn London apart attempting to find—was not the mistress to Lord Sundenbury at all. Rather, she was the hellraising lord's sister.

For the first fortnight after her disappearance, Dom had done everything in his power to wring the truth from the spoiled lordling he had sworn to protect. He may have been born in the rookery and raised in the seamy alleyways of the East End, and he may have cut his teeth picking pockets and running confidence schemes, but every leader in the rookeries had his word and his honor.

Without either of those, a man was nothing.

And so, Dom had continued to protect Sundenbury, upholding his end of the bargain with the angel who had so enthralled him and then betrayed him by slipping out of his gaming hell when he had been asleep, never to return. But he had seen the recognition in his quarry's face, at long last, when Dom had outright inquired after his angel, reminding

Sundenbury of the heavy price she had paid to secure his safety. Though the lord had continued to claim he was not currently keeping a mistress, Dom had not missed the moment of dawning comprehension, followed by abject horror.

Dom had witnessed such a look on a man's face before. Usually, it occurred when he was squaring off against an enemy and feared certain death. He had forced himself to have patience. To wait out Sundenbury until he would once more find himself in Dom's debt.

Three-and-forty days had been the precise number.

That had been how long it had been until Lord Sundenbury had sunk himself too deep at the green baize—little did he know Dom had aided him in his losses—and had confessed the truth. The angel of mercy who had visited Dom those fateful evenings had not been the despicable lordling's mistress at all.

No, indeed.

The next order of business had been, naturally, to discover the whereabouts of the lady in question. Sadly, not London.

Even worse, she was currently a guest at a country house party being hosted by none other than Mr. Deveraux Winter, Dom's despised half sibling. The gods were laughing at him. Vengeful, evil, despicable bastards that they were.

While Dom shared a father with Devereaux Winter, they most certainly shared nothing else save a name, and the name had only been down to Dom's determination all his half siblings should be united. They had different mothers—all of them save Gavin and Genevieve.

But where Devereaux Winter and his five sisters had been born to a life of privilege as the legitimate children of an incredibly wealthy merchant, Dom and his siblings had been the by-blows. The sources of prodigious *shame*. Easily ignored and forgotten. They had been the children abandoned to the terrifying streets, the ones who had been forced to scrabble and claw for everything they had. Dom had united them, and to say the bastard Winters loathed their counterparts was putting it mildly.

Rage was a festering, open sore.

But the gods who had placed Lady Adele at Devereaux Winter's house party would soon cease their laughter. Because Dom had formed a plan. All he needed to secure its execution was one thing.

Her.

The angel who had haunted his dreams. The only woman he had ever slept beside, trusting as a babe. And what good had his stupid trust gotten him? Waking to an empty bed and the mystery of a woman who did not exist. Lady Adele had not slipped a blade between his ribs that day as many an enemy would love to do, but she may as well have.

And now?

Now, she was going to help him get everything that had been eluding his grasp. Herself included.

At long last, through the swirling flurries against an overcast sky, the carriage approached a sprawling old manor house. The thing was impossibly large. So, too, the space of the outdoors all around him. Dom had been marveling over the vast expanses of countryside between villages ever since his first foray from the comforting boundaries of London had first begun.

Where London was all brick and buildings, tenements and wharves and factories and leaden skies and fog, the country was…almost an innocent cousin. Dom was envious of the cousin, but he bloody well did not want to spend forever at the cousin's side. He longed for the East End he had grown to love and hate, the streets and men he ruled, the dark alleyways where his name instilled fear into the hearts of so many.

In London, Dominic Winter was *someone*. An important, feared, impressive someone.

In the freezing, snow-bound landscape of the country, he was just another gent traveling to a house party. So innocuous was his presence that a youth had attempted to filch his coin at the last coaching inn where he had stayed. Dom had caught the bugger, forced him to return the coin, and brought him along for the remainder of the trip to Oxfordshire. There was always room for one more buzgloak—pickpocket—in London and in Dom's employ. The little shite was riding on the box, shivering his arse off for his troubles, but he would find a fine life in Dom's service if he played by the rules.

Playing by the rules was all that was expected of a man—or woman or child, for that matter—in the rookeries, no matter how twisted, tangled, broken, or bent. But since Lady Adele had come of age on the fine side of London, where the world had no ills worse than an upended teacup, she would not know that.

She would soon.

The carriage rolled to a stop.

Dom did not even wait for anyone to open the door. He snatched up his favorite walking stick and threw the lever himself, before leaping to the snow-covered gravel. Cold winds buffeted him, the chill of flurries clinging to his cheeks and lashes, as he took in the edifice before him, which could have easily dominated an entire city street.

"Are ye sure we're at the right place, yournabs?" called the little thief from the box.

Dom growled. "I am sure. And if you do not want me to turn you upside down and empty your thieving pockets, you will shut your biscuit hole, lad."

Satisfied his conveyance—coachman, and unexpected guest included—would see their way to the stables, Dom hastened up the wide stairs dominating the front of the home. He reached the door amidst a gust of blustery wind that threatened to take his hat.

A stern-looking butler greeted him.

"Have you come upon some trouble, sir?" asked the supercilious servant.

Dom's nostrils flared and his grip on his walking stick—which just happened to possess a secret sword—tightened. "No trouble at all. I have come to call upon Mr. Winter."

The butler's gaze settled upon the inking on Dom's hand. "Mr. Winter is otherwise occupied at the moment, sir."

Well, bloody Christ. Dom had rather fancied he was bang up to the mark for this particular visit.

"I am a guest," he pressed. "Mr. Winter is having a party. With guests. Aye? Stands to reason he would see me, on account of me traveling so far from home."

And also on account of the blade he carried.

And his insuppressible need for Lady Adele Saltisford.

Anyone who stood in Dom's way was going to be swallowing his teeth and nursing a flesh wound. He wanted the angel who had deceived and betrayed him and disappeared, and he meant to have her.

She was his, and unbeknownst to her, she was going to help him gain the upper hand over the Suttons.

The butler drew his shoulders back. "I am sorry, sir, but we are not expecting any further guests for the wedding breakfast this morning."

"I am afraid you are wrong there." He flashed the bastard a wicked grin, and then Dom pushed past him, stalking into an impressively cavernous entry hall. "Where is he? I would hate to go searching. It will be easier if you tell me where to find him."

And her.

But Dom kept the identity of his true quarry to himself. His boots clicked on the floor, and the servant raced after him. More footsteps sounded. He did not need to look over his shoulder to confirm an impromptu army of servants had begun stalking him.

"I would not follow me if I were you," he called confidently. "I can be a dangerous man, when provoked."

Actually, he was dangerous when he was not provoked as well. Lethal, in fact. But no need to mention that to the gaggle of bumpkins following him now. The only trouble was, he had no notion of where he was going. This bloody mausoleum was massive. One could house an entire London street within it, for the love of all that was…

He spotted some servants bearing trays up ahead, and he followed his instinct. And his nose—he scented food. Which meant there was a dining hall somewhere in the vicinity, and presumably within, Mr. Devereaux Winter and all his aristocratic guests.

"Sir, please," called the butler. "I command you to stop."

Dom laughed. If only the hapless fool knew he was addressing one of the most powerful men in London. But never mind, for someone dared to grab his coat sleeve. Dom did not hesitate. He spun, determining the aggressor was a strapping young footman, and took aim, his fist connecting with the unfortunate fellow's chin.

"Anyone else?" he demanded of the gathering crowd.

Slack jaws and silence met his query.

"I thought not."

With confidence, he turned about and reached what he suspected was the dining hall. He threw the double doors open. Within, a table, flanked with lords and ladies—and his hated half brother—was laden with delicacies. But Dom did not give a goddamn about any of the foods or the guests. All he cared about was one deceptive brunette goddess. His gaze lit upon her.

There she was, more beautiful than he recalled. Dressed to perfection in a gown of cream, as if she were truly the angel he had once believed her. Fury reverberated through him, along with a fierce, possessive rush.

Mine, whispered a voice inside him. *Fucking mine.*

As if she could hear his thoughts, she gasped.

Behind him, all the flurry of footsteps which had been trailing his progress arrived. The butler apologized profusely to the gathering before turning his attention back to Dom.

"Sir, I am going to have to ask you to leave," he said, raising a sanctimonious brow.

Pompous prick.

Dom raised his walking stick and withdrew the hollow end of it to reveal his hidden blade. "I've already silenced one of you with my fists. If I am forced to silence another, I'll not be responsible for the bloodshed."

One of the fancy coves at the table stood suddenly, and all the rest followed suit.

"What the devil are you doing here?" demanded a voice Dom just barely recognized from their one and only meeting some years prior.

Devereaux Winter had only discovered he possessed a bounty of illegitimate half siblings after their arsehole father's death. Their father's will had apparently given away his sordid secrets. Winter had done exactly what Dom would have expected of a fancy cove. He had come to The Devil's Spawn to attempt to buy Dom and the rest of the illegitimate Winters.

Dom had told him to bugger off. The money was unwanted. So, too, the familial connection.

"Forgive me," he told his half brother, scorn dripping from his voice. "It looks as if I have interrupted a wedding breakfast. My invitation must have been lost."

Devereaux Winter looked as if he wanted to commit murder. He gripped the back of his chair, scowling. "You are not welcome on my lands."

That was rich.

"Your lands?" Dom mocked, raising a brow. "Ah, yes, you bought it just as you buy everything and everyone."

The enmity between them was old and incurable. Only one goal could have driven Dom here. His pride was too great to ever come calling upon Devereaux bloody Winter. Damn the man to Hades.

"Why the hell are you here?" his half brother demanded.

Ah, an easy answer. Dom's gaze traveled to Lady Adele Saltisford once more, taking grim note that she had paled considerably. Indeed, she looked as if she had seen a ghost. Or as if she needed to cast up her accounts.

"I have come for what is mine," he told Lady Adele before flicking his gaze back to his half brother. "At long last."

"Nothing here is yours," Devereaux warned him.

"I suppose blood means nothing to you," Dom countered, unperturbed.

That was the thing about them—he and Devereaux Winter were drastically different.

"Go back to the rookeries where you belong," his half brother snapped. "I will not allow you to hurt this family."

"I have no intention of hurting anyone as long as I get what I have come here for." Dom's lip curled. "Fear not. The bastard Winters want no part of any of you. Attempt to become an aristocrat all you like. We earn our coin as we see fit and answer to no one, least of all Devereaux Winter."

"We need to speak," his half brother announced grimly. "In private."

Fair enough. But Dom had no intention of leaving without doing what he had journeyed all this way for. Still, he could play the civilized gentleman when he chose.

To that end, he inclined his head and trailed in Devereaux Winter's wake as he left the dining hall. He was keenly aware of Lady Adele's eyes upon him, following his retreat.

She had not expected to find him here, on her own turf. But if she thought he was the sort of chap who was afraid to invade enemy territory, she knew nothing about the man she had cozened. Because Dominic Winter had no bloody fear, and that was why he had managed to seize the reins of London's stews and wrap half the East End around his little finger.

And when he left Oxfordshire, she was going to be accompanying him.

By fair means or foul.

❄

HE WAS *HERE*.

Dominic Winter.

Adele had not been prepared for the sight of him in the wilds of Oxfordshire, so far from London. She had hoped he would not remember her. That he would not look for her.

Yet, he had. There had been no mistaking the expression on his wickedly handsome face, the cruel promise in his stare. He had come for her, he knew the truth, and he was furious.

Her stomach tightened into a knot, and she feared she would cast up her accounts all over the lovely wedding breakfast. What a horrid guest she was, inviting herself to remain at Abingdon Hall after the Christmastide house party had ended. Then bringing Dominic Winter down upon them in the midst of the celebration for the nuptials of the Duke and Duchess of Coventry…

"Who the devil is he?" asked Mr. Merrick Hart, brother-in-law to the Winter siblings, looking bewildered as he surveyed the rest of the assemblage.

"He is Dominic Winter," Adele managed to say, "and I fear he has come here for me."

All eyes turned to her. *Drat.* She had said too much.

"Dominic *Winter*?" asked the Duchess of Coventry—formerly Miss Christabella Winter.

Her Grace was the wildest of all the Winter sisters, with the flaming curls and outspoken nature to prove it. She had become an unlikely friend for Adele during the course of the house party she had attended with her older sister Hannah and twin sister Evangeline. Adele had managed to extract Her Grace's aid in persuading Hannah to leave her behind for an extended visit without her sister's watchful eye.

Adele perfectly understood the nature of her friend's query. She wished she had an answer.

"Mr. Winter is an…acquaintance of my brother's," she elaborated. "A gaming hell owner. That is to say, I believe he is."

Heavens, it was unseemly for her to admit her knowledge of such an inappropriate connection. What had she been thinking? It was the shock of his appearance, after two long months, of the way he had looked at her…

As if he could see inside her.

The equal fear of her secret. A secret she must keep at all costs. A secret she would do anything, *anything* to protect. Including lying to her sisters and her newfound friend, the Duchess of Coventry.

For what seemed an eternity, no one spoke. Adele went

hot, then cold, a fine sheen of perspiration breaking out on her brow. Her stomach lurched. She could not be certain if the nausea churning was the same as that which had been ordinarily plaguing her or if it was a result of her current predicament.

Likely, a combination of both.

"Is he...could he be from a distant branch of our Winter family?" ventured Mrs. Merrick Hart.

"A disgraced portion," added the Duchess of Coventry. "He said 'bastard Winters,' did he not?"

"Christabella," chastised her elder sister, Lady Prudence Rawdon. "You ought to know better than to repeat such nonsense. Our reputations as Winters are bedeviled enough. No need to borrow trouble."

It was true. The Wicked Winters, as they were mockingly known within society, possessed untold wealth thanks to their merchant father's empire. What they had lacked was the requisite ties to high society until Mr. Devereaux Winter had married Lady Emilia King. Their *entrée* to the *ton* was new.

"How can I borrow trouble when it has already shown up, brandishing a sword hidden in a cane?" the duchess dared to ask.

Adele rolled her lips inward, fighting against a renewed wave of bile.

She had saved Max and ruined herself. And now, she had also brought ruin and mayhem down upon her new friend's wedding day.

She hated herself.

"It looked wickedly sharp," Miss Grace Winter said. "Do you think he has ever used it upon any of his enemies? I found myself looking for traces of blood..."

"Grace!" The chiding exclamation came from Miss Eugie Winter, who was engaged to wed the Earl of Hertford. "That is hardly proper discussion for Christabella's wedding breakfast. Let us return to our celebrations. I am certain our brother will conclude his business with this Mr. Winter as soon as possible and return."

More agony buffeted Adele.

The ominous arrival of Mr. Dominic Winter was all her fault.

Adele stood, sending her chair toppling to the floor. Once more, the eyes of the gathering were upon her. She wished the floor beneath her would open and swallow her, giving her the escape she so desperately needed.

But when you made a deal with the devil, he always demanded his due. Rather than allow the Duke and Duchess of Coventry's special day to suffer any further interruption, she would face her devil.

"Felicitations, Your Graces," she said. "I wish you both the best in your future together as husband and wife. If you will all excuse me, I find myself feeling quite ill, and I have no wish to burden the joyous gathering any more than I already have."

She dipped into a curtsy and fled from the dining hall as quickly as her pride would allow. Her stomach was indeed roiling as she made her way down the hall in search of Mr. Dominic Winter and Mr. Devereaux Winter. The same surname—the significance of it haunted her now. She had known, of course, the Winter who had changed her life two months before shared the same surname as the Winter who was playing her host at Abingdon Hall. However, sharing a name did not necessarily suggest a connection.

As she hastened down the hall, attempting to find out where her host Mr. Winter may have taken her Mr. Winter, she could not help but to think about the similarities between the two men. Both were tall, dark-haired, handsome, and large of frame. Muscled and monstrous.

She discovered a closed door and barreled through it, startled when she found both Mr. Winters in heated debate with each other. They paused, their gazes narrowing upon her. That was when she realized she had thought of Mr. Dominic Winter as *her* Mr. Winter. And that was also when she realized she was doomed.

She saw keenly the differences between the two men now—Dominic Winter exuded an aura of absolute danger. His dark hair was too long for fashion. His body appeared perpetually coiled, as if to strike at any moment. Her host, on the other hand, possessed a calm demeanor of command. It was plain to see neither Mister Winter liked the other.

"Lady Adele, this is a private matter," Mr. Devereaux Winter told her, breaking the silent exchange of stares.

"Forgive me for the interruption," she said, her cheeks going hot as she realized she was being despicably rude. Presumptuous too, to believe Dominic Winter would come here specifically for her. "I…mistook this chamber for another."

She turned to flee.

"Wait."

The deep, commanding voice of Dominic Winter stopped her when she would have flown from the room. Adele paused, looking back to the two men. His gaze clashed with hers, stealing all the breath from her lungs.

"As this is a matter which concerns you, Lady Adele," he elaborated smoothly, "you may as well stay."

"What can this possibly have to do with Lady Adele?" Mr. Devereaux Winter growled. "She is under my protection here at Abingdon Hall. Leave her out of whatever grievances you claim to have against my family."

"Your family?" Dominic Winter's lip curled. "I thought it

was *our* family, brother. Always so goddamn selfish, are you not?"

So it was true, then. The two men before her shared blood.

"I am not your brother," Devereaux Winter snapped.

"Half brother, brother, same difference, is it not?" Dominic Winter flashed a feral grin. "Our father liked to keep his prick wet, and he did not give a damn who was doing the wetting. Twelve children to show for his efforts. Quite impressive, I say."

Devereaux Winter's hands balled into fists. "You are speaking in the presence of a lady, you blackguard."

Dominic Winter's gaze returned to Adele, who had been watching the dialogue between the two men unfold, in shock at the revelations. "Is she a lady? Might be open to discussion, that."

She flinched at the insult he paid her. Yes, he was angry with her. She had spent the time since she had slipped from his chamber and his gaming hell fearing he would find out her true identity. That he would come looking for her. And that if he located her, all would be lost…

"Leave us, Lady Adele," Devereaux Winter told her gently. "There is no need to subject yourself to his wrath."

"I fear there is." Adele took a deep breath. "I need to speak to Mr. Winter. Alone."

Her host looked dumbfounded by her abrupt announcement. He frowned at her, his brow furrowed. "I beg your pardon, my lady?"

He was going to make her repeat herself.

Her ears went hot, and the churning in her stomach increased, the knot there tightening with almost painful intensity. "I must have an audience with Mr. Winter."

Mr. Devereaux Winter continued to frown, her repetition

of her request apparently doing nothing to quell his concern.

Dominic Winter was quicker to respond. "There now, you did not believe I came all this way to lick your boots, did you, brother? I hate to be the bearer of ill tidings, but I did not travel to Oxfordshire to watch you playing duke with your new wife and all your fancy cove friends. I came here for *her*."

His confirmation of her fears did nothing to soothe her inner turmoil.

"What business can an East End rat like you have with the daughter of a duke?" Devereaux Winter asked, his tone biting as the lash of a whip.

Her ordinarily genial host's bitterness was not lost upon Adele. The two men before her did not just dislike each other. They hated each other. And yet, if what Dominic Winter said was to be believed, they had the same father. Half brothers, so different and yet so much the same.

"Would you care to answer that question, love?" Dominic Winter taunted her.

For a searing moment, she remembered the way his lips felt against hers. The way he had brought her to life. The pleasure he had given her. How tender his touch had been. As if she had been fashioned of the finest porcelain. But where he once would have protected her from shattering, he was now on the path of imminent destruction, and it was Adele he meant to ruin.

"Mr. Winter was kind enough to aid my brother," Adele said, pleased with herself for keeping the tremble from her voice.

"See that, brother?" Dominic taunted. "The lady says I was kind. Now shove off so I can speak with her. She has something of mine, and I mean to get it back."

Adele did not argue with him before Devereaux Winter, but she had taken nothing from him. All she wanted to do was meet with Dominic Winter, settle whatever debts he believed she still owed him, and then disappear into the countryside forever, as had been her original plan.

"It will be hasty, Mr. Winter," Adele said. "A mere ten minutes, nothing more."

Devereaux Winter looked from her to Dominic, his countenance reflecting his bafflement. "Ten minutes," he allowed, reluctance edging his voice. "No more, and I will be in the hall, with the door ajar. If he dares anything, I will be here, Lady Adele."

Chapter Seven

"WE MEET AGAIN."

His silken voice was deceptively calm. His eyes, however, blazed with dark fury.

Dominic Winter was not pleased. In fact, he was furious. With her.

Adele swallowed and forced herself to square her shoulders as he prowled toward her, stopping too near for propriety's sake. She would not wilt before him. Would not bend. "I confess, I am surprised to see you at this particular country house party, Mr. Winter."

His sensual lips twisted into a sneer. "I go where I please, as it pleases me. I do not give a bloody shite about half brothers who think they are the quality because they are swiving the daughter of a duke."

Dom's rough words took her aback. "Mr. Devereaux Winter is married to Lady Emilia."

Dom shrugged. "Married or not, he is still swiving her."

She frowned at him. "You are being deliberately crude."

"No, love. I am being deliberately dismissive." His lip curled even farther. "Because I don't give a damn about Winter or his ladybird. I came here for you, and you know it."

Yes, she did.

Adele suppressed a shiver. His words both filled her with anticipation and dread, all at once. She did not know how to manage a Dominic Winter who was this angry. Particularly not one who had ventured to the countryside in the midst of frigid winter, leaving London and his empire of crime behind.

Surely he could not suspect. There was no reason for him to know the truth of her carefully guarded secret. He had chased her here because he had discovered her lie and he was angry about it. That had to be the answer. Imagine, a well-bred lady fooling the devilish Dominic Winter, the most feared man in London.

"Why would you come here for me?" she dared to ask.

His eyes were stormy and intent upon hers. "You know why, Duchess."

"You discovered who I am and it displeases you," she guessed.

He laughed, the sound bitter. Cutting. "I did indeed. Lady Adele Saltisford. Sister to Lord Sundenbury. Not mistress."

She hated the way he was looking at her now, the wrath lacing his voice. "I am Lady Adele, yes. However, I never suggested to you that I was anything other than myself. If you presumed—"

"If I presumed," he bit out, interrupting her, "and you did not correct my presumption, then you lied to me, *Lady Adele.*"

"I did not lie," she argued quietly, also despising the manner in which he referred to her, as if her title and name were an epithet that tasted bitter upon his tongue.

"You allowed me to believe you were Sundenbury's mistress," he hissed. "That was a lie."

"I never said I was his mistress."

But even as she offered her protest to the contrary, she knew how hollow it sounded. Because Dominic Winter was right, of course. She had misled him. And she may as well have lied to him. But her reasoning had been sound, her motivation pure.

"You also never said you were not," he said coolly.

The way he was watching her made her want to flee. Oh, what this man did to her. He undid her. Without fail.

"I came to you with the express hope of seeing to my brother's safety," she forced herself to counter. "If you drew erroneous conclusions, I cannot be blamed for them. My objective was in making certain no more of your ruffians hurt my brother. I accomplished my aim, and I will not apologize for it."

"And I have made certain Sundenbury has been safe, have I not?" He cocked his head, surveying her, his eyes sweeping over her form in a way that made her feel uneasy and scorching hot all at once.

Her brother was safe. Adele, however, was not. She had never been more certain of that than she was now. There was no one here to save her. Oh, she could raise a cry and Mr. Devereaux Winter, not far, would rush to her aid. But nothing stopped a man like Dominic Winter from getting what he wanted.

"I paid dearly for it," she countered. "I owe you nothing now, Mr. Winter."

"Once, you called me Dom," he reminded her, his perusal taking on a far more sensual quality. "You moaned it, in fact. While you were in my bed. Do you remember?"

Her ears went hot. She was flushed, from head to toe. Of course she remembered. She had thought of nothing else since. The memory of his touch haunted her. She longed for him. Ached for him. But she was no fool. There could be no future between Lady Adele Saltisford and London's most dangerous crime lord.

"You are vulgar, sir, and I need not subject myself to more of your taunts." She moved to leave, but he stayed her, catching her elbow in a firm grasp.

"I can be much more vulgar than this, love."

His voice was laden with dark promise and wicked intent.

The same part of her that had been drawn to him before burst into flame. Adele wanted to kiss him and run from him, all at once.

"Did you truly journey to Oxfordshire in the midst of winter to take me to task for misleading you?" she demanded, cursing herself for the breathlessness in her voice.

For her reaction to him, the awareness flaring to life like a slow and steady flame bound to consume her. Why had she ever believed she could bargain with a man like Dominic Winter?

❄

TWO LONG MONTHS of scouring London to find her. An equal amount of time spent ensuring his plan would succeed. One treacherous journey to the country. An unpleasant interview with his arsehole of a half brother. It had all led Dom to this moment. Victory would soon be his, in more than one sense. The first was here and now; the second would come later.

Lady Adele Saltisford was close enough to touch.

Her scent wrapped around him. Her lips tempted him. *Soon*, he promised himself. *Cling to your anger. Show her what happens when you make a fool of Dominic Winter.*

"Of course I did not come all this way to take you to task." He could not resist reaching out and touching her.

Just a skim of his bare fingers on her jaw. The contact between them gave him the same rare jolt it had two months ago.

Curse her.

"I am here because your brother has once again been plagued with ill luck at the tables," he drawled. Never mind that he had made certain of it. She was not the only one who excelled at keeping secrets. "He is in a great deal of debt, and his safety is in jeopardy."

She went pale. "How much debt?"

"Twenty thousand pounds."

"I cannot repay you as I did before," she rushed to say. "I should never have done so then."

"I did not ask for your services now did I, Duchess?" He was being cruel and he knew it. But a man who had mercy on the streets was a man who had nothing. "Before you deny me, mayhap you want to hear the cost."

"There can be no cost." She stepped away from him, severing their connection at last. "I have nothing left to say to you, Mr. Winter."

The hell she did not.

They had only just begun, Dominic Winter and Lady Adele Saltisford.

Dom chased her, catching her elbow once more and staying her when she would have fled the room. "A handsome cove, your brother. Do you think the ladies will still fancy him if he has but one eye instead of two? Or one hand? Fingers are easily broken or cut off. Toes, now those are a deuced thorny proposition. Cut off the wrong one, and a man loses his balance forever. Left Leg Louis has never been the same since it happened to him, not even after the cobbler fixed him special crabshells."

Her eyes widened. "Crabshells?"

"Shoes, Duchess." He flashed her a slow, grim smile. The one he gave to the men who betrayed him just before he ground them to dust beneath his boot heel.

"Y-you would not do my brother such violence," she

protested. "You would be arrested."

"I don't do violence," he purred, leaning nearer to her. So near, their lips almost brushed. "I have men who do it for me. And as for me being under arrest...I own the streets and all who govern them."

He recognized the swell of fear in her lovely countenance. Ordinarily, terrorizing his opponent was the source of eminent joy. This enemy, however, was different. All he felt was a hollowness inside his chest, a gaping chasm threatening to swallow him whole.

And still, she remained stoic. Brave and defiant. Here was the same lady who had dared to enter his lair, who had stood before him and made a bargain he had failed to realize involved the surrendering of her innocence.

She did not flinch, nor tear her eyes from his. "You cannot own everyone, Mr. Winter. You are not above the law."

How little she knew of the world. Her naiveté was almost charming.

He cocked his head, studying her, wishing her beauty did not affect him. "I reckon I could make Prinny dance a jig if I asked nicely enough."

Dom had risen to power through might, determination, violence, money, and blackmail. Not necessarily in that order. He felt no guilt for the sins in which he had engaged. The world was corrupt; he was merely using that corruption to benefit himself, his family, and his men.

"I do not believe you," she insisted. "No man is that powerful."

"Wrong again, Duchess. Not every man is that powerful. But *I* am. You would do well to remember it, because when I am your husband, if you dare to betray me, you will suffer the consequences."

Her eyes, fringed with sooty lashes that were longer than

he had recalled, widened even more. "Husband?"

Not quite the manner in which he had intended to announce his price for her brother's continued safety. The next part of his strategy, about to unfold. But he had already blown the gaff. No undoing it now.

"Why else did you suppose I would come all the way to Oxfordshire to collect you?" he asked coolly. "Sundenbury is all cleaned out; you have reached your majority. Your hand in marriage is the price I am demanding to cancel his debts."

"You want to marry me?" If possible, more color leached from her cheeks. Her breath was a hot, tempting fan over his lips.

Christ, even her breath was sweet. Like honey.

He wanted to devour her.

"I am going to marry you, Duchess," he corrected.

"No."

He must have misheard her. No one told Dominic Winter *no*. "I beg your pardon?"

"No, I cannot marry you," she repeated.

Foolish Lady Adele. There was no choice. From the moment she had willingly placed herself within his grasp, she had sealed her fate.

He raised a brow. "You are already married to another?"

She frowned. "No, of course not."

"Then you can and will marry me. Problem solved, Duchess."

Devereaux Winter chose that moment to return, barreling through the door with the grace of an invading army. There was no love lost between Dom and his half brother, but the arsehole could have selected better timing. Lady Adele all but tripped over her own hems in her effort to put some distance between herself and Dom.

"Your ten minutes is over," Devereaux announced acidly.

Dom was going to have far more than ten minutes.

But there was time enough to execute his plan. And for now, he would settle for ruffling the protective feathers of brother dearest, who did not like an East End gutter rat sniffing so near to his pristine sisters and fine guests.

He slapped his strapping half brother on the back as if he were a lad. "One more mouth to feed shouldn't be trouble for a man with your blunt, brother. I've been wearing the bands all day, I have."

Dom relished the way Devereaux Winter stiffened and frowned at his use of cant. It pleased him to displease brother dearest.

"Wearing the bands?" Devereaux repeated, his lip curling.

"Hungry," Dom translated. "Looked like a wedding breakfast I interrupted. Just the thing. Don't fret over me. I'll be quiet as a thief filching the family silver."

An apt description, that. The expression on both his half brother and Lady Adele's faces told him so.

"You cannot remain here," brother dearest said.

Predictably.

"Aye, I can." He tapped his walking stick on the floor as a pointed reminder of what was hidden within. "And I will. You'll not turn out your own blood when I have newly arrived. Besides, I am thinking you will want to celebrate my betrothal to Lady Adele."

The arsehole's scowl was instant and thunderous. "What the devil?"

"We are not betrothed," Lady Adele protested simultaneously.

"A mere formality," he said, giving her a wink. "We cannot keep the secret to ourselves forever, love. May as well share the good news."

"Mr. Winter," she snapped, her mouth a disapproving

line.

He was pushing her. Prodding her. It was almost entertaining, toying with the woman as he was. She deserved everything he was giving her and more. So much more, damn her. The effrontery of the chit, a bloody duke's daughter, deceiving the feared Dominic Winter. If the East End ever discovered the fool she had made of him, one of his enemies would topple him from his throne in a goddamn stroke of the clock.

"You are not engaged to Lady Adele," brother dearest countered then, as if his decree would make it so.

"What?" He clucked his tongue the way his ma had done whenever he had done something naughty as a lad. "You do not think you are the only Winter who can marry himself a duke's daughter, do you?"

Color tinged Devereaux Winter's cheekbones. It was the shade of rage.

Floating hell, how good it felt to nettle this steaming pile of donkey shit.

"I have no proof you are a Winter," Devereaux bit out curtly.

When Winter had first discovered the existence of Dom and his five siblings at the reading of their father's will, he had been shocked. He had also been skeptical. And that, more than any other reason, had been why Dom had told brother dearest to shove the inheritance where the sun did not dare shine.

Up his lily-white arse.

Dom shrugged at him now, grinning. "Don't need to prove anything to a nib."

"You are not attending my sister's wedding breakfast," his half brother growled at him.

"And why not? She is my sister too." As if Dom gave a

bloody damn. They were not true family, nor would they ever be.

Which was fine by him. The bastard Winters did not need the fancy Winters. They never had. Their worlds were far too different.

"Until today, she did not know you existed, which is how it should have remained," brother dearest snarled.

"I fear I must return to my chamber, sirs," came the dulcet, smooth voice of Lady Adele. "I have a megrim."

Dom's gaze flew to her, but she was keeping her eyes trained in studious fashion upon the toes of her slippers as she dipped into a curtsy.

"We will speak later, love," he told her, equal parts promise and threat.

They were far from through. She could fight him all she liked, but he always got what he wanted in the end. He would not be thwarted or defeated. He was going to take Lady Adele Saltisford as his wife.

And then, he was going to have the Suttons at his mercy.

His future wife said nothing, merely disappeared from the room.

Dom did not miss the stricken expression on her face, the look in her eyes which was akin to a man who knew his end was imminent. He was going to have to find his way to her room. And soon.

But first, he had a half brother to rankle.

And a wedding breakfast to attend.

He thumped Devereaux Winter on the back once again with more force than necessary. "Lead on, brother. It is not every day that my sister is wed."

"I am going to kill you," his nemesis threatened.

Dom grinned. "I would love to see you try."

Perverse bastard that he was, he meant every word.

Chapter Eight

SHE SHOULD HAVE run when she had the chance.

No, instead Adele had remained at Abingdon Hall, wanting to see her friend marry the Duke of Coventry. And now she had been caught, just like any mouse about to be devoured by a starving cat. But first the cat would toy with her, paw at her, make her misery its first course.

Yes, she thought as she paced the carpets of her chamber, attempting to assemble some manner of battle plan, Dominic Winter was a vicious cat. A lion, more like. And he was intent upon doing to her what he wished until there was nothing left.

She would not marry him.

Could not marry him.

He was a violent man. A man who had blithely threatened to have one of his henchmen take Max's eye or cut off one of his toes. A criminal who had already made her barter her brother's safety with her body two months ago.

But he was also the man who had kissed her so sweetly, who had visited intense pleasure, the likes of which she had never supposed existed, upon her body. He was the man for whom she had longed, in all the days since she had seen him last. The man she had dreaded. The man she wanted despite all sound logic and reason.

He was the man who had ruined her.

The father of her unborn babe.

She cradled her abdomen now, the small swell, barely there. The slightest hint she was no longer the innocent girl who had gone to The Devil's Spawn in hopes of keeping her brother from suffering another beating. The smallest sign there was a new life within her. Dominic Winter must never discover she was carrying his child.

"No," she said aloud, hugging her midsection as she paced, "he must never, ever know."

"What must I never know, Duchess?"

She jumped on a shriek, whirling about to face the source of that low, most unwanted baritone. There, in the shadows of her chamber, stood Dominic Winter. Tall, dark, dangerous.

Handsome.

Too handsome.

How in heaven's name had he gained entry to her private space? She had barred the door and windows. How had he known she was talking about him?

She pressed a hand to her wildly thumping heart, willing it to calm. "What are you doing in my chamber, Mr. Winter?"

"Are we back to the formalities?" He slowly sauntered toward her, as if he had all the time in the world with which to approach. "I confess, I miss hearing you call me Dom."

"Remove yourself from this room at once," she ordered him, blustering.

Because she was a defenseless woman half his size, and he was a towering wall of conscienceless muscle.

"No. Don't reckon I shall." He kept moving toward her, his long-legged strides eating up the distance separating them with ease.

"Why are you still at Abingdon Hall?" she demanded, for she had hoped Mr. Devereaux Winter would simply evict his alleged half brother from the grounds and send him back to

London. That she could hide away until he was gone and she was safe to continue with her plans.

That would have been far too easy, however.

And she should have known better. Dominic Winter would never allow himself to be dismissed.

He reached her, looping his arms around her waist, then hauling her against his body. They were flush, her breasts crushed to his chest, her hips snugly fitted to his. He lowered his head so their faces were painfully close. She felt every part of him. Including the thick ridge of his manhood.

An answering heat slid through her, settling between her thighs.

"I am still at Abingdon Hall because Devereaux Winter's bark is far worse than his bite." He flashed her a wicked smile. "He hasn't the ballocks to attempt to run me from here, for fear of the blood that would be shed."

She swallowed. "Blood?"

Adele wanted to believe he would not harm anyone. That his words had been chosen to frighten.

But Dominic Winter was not the most feared man in London without reason. The lover who had touched her with such gentle skill was also a ruthless murderer and unrepentant criminal. A man who would kiss sweetly one moment and threaten to cut off a man's hand and toes the next. He was the darkness. She was the light.

Persephone and Hades, that was what they were.

But Adele had no intention of allowing Hades to spirit her away. He could return to rule his underworld without her.

"I see your pretty mind spinning like the wheels on a carriage," he said then, reaching out to run a lone finger down her forehead, as if he could smooth the furrow from her brow. "You are telling yourself I would never hurt the Winters, since we are family. You are wrong, however. I am a dangerous man, and I do not smile upon those who betray me or go against me."

Those who betray me.

The warning sounded as if it had been made purely for her sake. "I did not betray you, Mr. Winter."

The roughened pad of his forefinger traveled lower in the softest of touches, skimming along the bridge of her nose. "It is Dom, Duchess. And yes, you did."

He was warning her. His presence in Oxfordshire—his presence within her chamber—it had all been cleverly calculated and planned. Adele suspected he was a man who did not settle upon a course lightly.

"How did I betray you?" she asked, gasping as his finger dipped lower, to her lips.

But still, he traced the outline of them, staying away from her seam, never once rubbing over her mouth itself. It was a careful game of avoidance he played. For a man who seemed so wild and unpredictable, his every move was executed with incredible deliberation. Every look, word, touch meant *something*.

"You lied to me, and you slipped away from my bed while I was sleeping." His dark gaze was upon her lips.

They tingled, as if his stare was itself a touch.

She had to gird herself against this man's mesmerizing power. Against his potent allure. He was not for her. Far better to flee, to find a situation in the country. A quiet cottage. To raise her babe far away from his dangerous world.

"We have been through this already," she forced herself to say. "I never lied. I merely failed to correct your assumption. And as for leaving you whilst you slept, what else was I to have done? Remained forever? I had already put myself and my reputation in enough danger by going to you twice."

"You lied about something else as well, Duchess." His

finger trailed down her throat, and then he slid his hand to cup her nape, the touch as soft as velvet. "You made me believe you were an experienced seductress instead of an innocent maid. You might have warned me, you know. I would have been gentler for your first time."

His assertion took her by surprise. So, too, his caress. The hand at her nape was like a brand, burning her with wicked intent. She was falling beneath this man's spell again. How did he do it?

She swallowed, wishing the desire unfurling within her could be dispelled. Wishing she could shake this most inconvenient attraction to him. What was wrong with her, wanting a criminal who threatened her brother with polished ease?

"I do not want to speak about what happened," she forced out, stepping away from him, severing their contact.

She needed distance between them. An entire vast sea, if possible.

"We won't talk about it then." He pursued her, following her to the window at the opposite end of the chamber.

Wrong choice, Adele.

She ought to have gone toward the door, all the better to make her escape. Was jumping from the window a sensible option?

"You have no right to be in my chamber," she countered as he flattened his palms on either side of her, trapping her.

Although the cold seeped through the windowpane at her back, Adele was aflame.

He lowered his head so their lips were disturbingly near once more. "I have every right. You are my future wife."

"I am not marrying you."

"Yes." He kissed the corner of her lips. "You are, Duchess."

"I am the daughter of a duke, not the wife of one," she blurted, her mind whirling as if she had just spun about in a dozen circles. "I am not a duchess."

He made her feel dizzied and overheated.

And confused.

"I know what you are." He kissed the other corner of her mouth, then her cheek. "Even rats from the East End know the difference between a duchess and the daughter of one."

"Mr. Winter ought not to have spoken so harshly," she managed.

He had kissed his way to her ear now. Adele could not suppress the shiver that went down her spine. He was making her weak, with his proximity and his wicked mouth. It was not fair that a man like him should be so beautiful, so tempting, that he could kiss and touch and caress her to the point she forgot the difference between right and wrong.

"Brother dearest is right." He kissed her neck. "I *am* a rat from the rookeries."

She flattened her hands on his chest, but instead of pushing him away, her fingers had curled into the soft fabric of his shirt. She was holding him there, tilting her head, resting it upon the iced pane behind her.

"But why are you here?" she forced herself to ask. "Why are you not in London?"

He smiled against her skin. "Because my little bird flew away, and I had to find her so I can bring her back to me where she belongs."

"I do not belong in your world." Her eyes slid closed as he sucked on her flesh as if he could devour her.

"You do now." The sharp brush of his teeth against her collarbone sent a spark of painful pleasure through her. "I am claiming you."

It was difficult to think with his big body surrounding

her, his scent enveloping her. He was turning her insides into honey. She wanted him to claim her. She wanted everything he was saying, each touch, his mouth on her, his hands. All the reasons why she should not succumb to him dissipated beneath his potent seduction.

Sternly, she summoned them to return. "I do not want to be claimed."

"You should have thought about that before you came to The Devil's Spawn and made a bargain with the devil himself." His lips moved lower, traveling over her breasts. "Do you want to save your brother, Duchess, or do you want to be stubborn?"

She wanted to be stubborn and safe and far from this man. But she also wanted to make certain Max remained unharmed. And she could not deny that she wanted Dominic Winter's kisses. A wicked, restless part of her *wanted* him to claim her.

He tugged on her bodice, and her breasts sprang free of her stays. Cool air kissed them, her nipples hard and throbbing. Adele could not form an answer as he took one in his mouth and sucked. Liquid heat shot from her breast to the apex of her thighs.

Her knees went weak, but when she would have melted into a puddle on the floor, he held her against the window. The contrast between the cold, slick glass at her back and the heated man filling her with so much fire only heightened her awareness.

His tongue flicked over the peak of her breast.

She told herself this was wrong. That she did not dare trust Dominic Winter.

But then the door to her chamber flew open, and an angry shout and a feminine gasp of outrage echoed through the room, above the mad pounding of her heart. Dom swiftly tugged her bodice back into place, covering her.

The grin he flashed her was undeniably smug. "I reckon your decision has been made for you, love."

One glimpse at the grim countenances of her host and hostess over Dominic Winter's shoulder proved him right. Her heart plummeted to the soles of her slippers.

Chapter Nine

"I WANT YOUR promise, Mr. Winter."

Foolish chit. She was utterly lovely in her cream gown with a scarlet sash beneath her generous bosom. Her eyes flashed with fire, her proud chin tilted up in challenge. Did she still think she possessed any of the power in this little tragedy of theirs? She would discover the difference soon enough.

Dom raised a brow, allowing his gaze to sweep from her head to her toes. "Has no one ever told you promises can be broken?"

"If you break your promise to me, I will be the one who carves out your eye," she told him, her bravado in fine form today, the day of their wedding.

"Before you issue threats, make certain you have the ballocks to uphold them," he counseled his almost-wife.

His almost-wife *at last*.

Impossible to believe he had been moldering in the monkery for three bloody weeks, waiting to wed this stubborn chit. He was a Bedlamite. Had to be. She was hardly worth the trouble.

Yes, countered a voice within him, *she is, you arse. She will give you everything you need to defeat the Suttons.*

Well, mayhap she was.

There was also the matter of how much he wanted her.

Brother dearest had done everything aside from place an armed guard outside her chamber door to keep Dom from his intended. Being so near to her and having to spend each evening fucking his hand had decidedly lost its luster. He could not wait to be inside her. And he intended to be so, just as soon as this godforsaken ceremony was through.

Devil and Blade had best be managing in his absence. He had never been gone from London for this long. He had not dared.

"Do you think I do not have the courage to stand up to you?" she demanded.

Damn, she was fierce. It was making him hard.

He adjusted his stance. No sense tenting his breeches before a man of the cloth. In a church. He was vile, but he had some sense of right and wrong. Or, at least, he once had. Over the years, that understanding had grown decidedly murkier and murkier.

Until he had forced a duke's daughter into marrying him, the bastard son of a Covent Garden doxy and a coldhearted merchant.

"I think your courage is admirable, Duchess," he said then, stroking his jaw. "If misplaced. I am not your enemy. I will be your husband."

"I do not understand why a man like you would want to wed." She shook her head, as if the motion would somehow force clarity upon her. "Marrying me will not gain you *entrée* in society."

He laughed. "Do you think I give a fuck about twirling around ballrooms and bowing and scraping to a gaggle of preening, pompous lords and their arrogant wives, sons, and daughters?"

She flinched at his coarse language. "I am sure I do not know anything you *do* care about, Mr. Winter."

To spite him, she had refused to refer to him as his given name for the entirety of their betrothal. Never mind that. He fully intended to make her moan it later.

"I care about marrying you, else I would not have traveled to the midst of nowhere and suffered the reluctant hospitality of an arsehole for three weeks."

That much was true.

He *did* care about marrying her. But the reason why was his affair and not hers.

"Mr. Winter was kind in allowing us to remain after the manner in which you interrupted the Duke and Duchess of Coventry's wedding breakfast and the…disgrace which happened thereafter." She was frowning at him again.

And pale. Her complexion matched her dress.

"Are you feeling well, Duchess?" he asked, concern for her swirling through him.

A new sensation, that. He had never cared about anyone other than his siblings before, had he? Ruthlessly, he tamped it down. There was no room for weakness in his world.

"I am fine, aside from the fact that I am being forced to marry a criminal against my will," she said sweetly.

"Are you certain?" he prodded, ignoring her insult for the moment. "You look as if you are going to be sick."

Her lips compressed. "Perfectly."

"I ain't a criminal these days, Duchess," he could not resist pointing out then. Her poor opinion of him rather nettled. "And nor is anyone forcing you into this marriage. You made the decision, all on your own."

Her nostrils flared. "Just because you pay others to commit crimes on your behalf does not mean you are not a criminal yourself. As for making the decision to marry you, you made certain I was left without a choice. If I do not marry you, I am not just ruined, but my brother will be harmed by you and your vicious minions."

Sundenbury again, that twat. At least he had proven useful, in the end.

"I encouraged you to make the right choice." Dom raised his hands, as if to show her his munificence. "There is no evidence I pay anyone to commit crimes on my behalf."

"Because you also pay the magistrates," she charged.

Clever woman, his future wife. That would prove a boon, he hoped, rather than a burden.

He shrugged. "What was the promise you wish to extract from me, Duchess? I will consider agreeing to your request because I am feeling…what would a fancy nib say? Magnanimous. Aye, I'm feeling magnanimous. On account of me soon being a married man and all."

She sighed. "I want you to promise me my brother will be safe. And I also want you to swear you will bar him from your establishment so he cannot lose any more funds. I want him forever free of debt to you."

Her love for her worthless brother was almost admirable. Except it was misplaced. As was her belief in him. Lady Adele Saltisford knew nothing of the ways of men or gamblers. It was almost sweet, her insistence she believe the best of Sundenbury.

Sweet? *Floating hell*, what was the matter with him? Brother dearest had likely slipped poison into the wassail.

"You truly think if I refuse him at The Devil's Spawn that he will not go elsewhere to have his pockets fleeced?" he asked her.

Lady Adele did not flinch, nor did she waiver. "I believe it will be a deterrent, especially after he realizes the extent of the sacrifice I made for him."

She was a rarity, this woman he was going to marry. She was dipped in sunshine and the foolish belief everyone around her was good. The truth was, every last one of them, from brother dearest down to the footmen, was fucking horrible. What must it be like, such unending, misplaced belief in the innate goodness of others?

For a moment, Dom wished he shared in her delusions.

Until he remembered where they would leave him—dead in an alleyway, a Sutton bullet lodged in his back.

"Ah, my darling duchess." He stroked the backs of his fingers down her silken cheek, the first touch he had permitted himself since meeting her in the library at her request. "I do hate to dismantle your idealism, but that is not the way of it for men who throw away their lives and fortunes upon the next flip of a card or roll of the dice. If I deny him, Sundenbury will go elsewhere, and he will lose his coin there all the same. Only, it will go worse for him as the owners of other establishments will not be members of his family."

In truth, there was no chance her brother would be admitted anywhere else. Dom had made it known in the East End that Sundenbury must be refused at all hells except The Devil's Spawn or risk facing retaliation from the Winters. He wanted the heir to the Duke of Linross in his debt, and not in the debt of any other. He would have Linross in the palm of his hand by more than one means, just where he needed him. And he would emerge victorious over the Suttons at last.

"Nonetheless, I demand your promise," she said.

Her determination was another trait to admire. It was also the reason why he had paid all brother dearest's servants to keep him apprised of her every move. He had foiled no fewer than six attempts to flee, all without her knowledge.

Lady Emilia Winter appeared at the threshold of the library. "The two of you will have an abundance of time to discuss what you wish in privacy after you wed."

If Lady Emilia believed there would be any discussion

following his marriage to Lady Adele, she was cut from the same foolish cloth.

But she was not wrong about her wish to get the marriage underway. The sooner Lady Adele was his, the better.

He turned back to his bride. "Very well, I give you my promise."

He said it with ease because he had no intention of holding true to his promise. That was yet another lesson his future wife had to learn. Never trust someone who wants something from you.

She searched his gaze, apparently seeing what she wanted there before she nodded. "I will do it."

With a curtsy, she turned and fled from the library, following Lady Emilia Winter.

In no time at all, he was going to be a married man.

And then, no one—not even Jasper Sutton and his army of bloodthirsty thieves—could stop the bastard Winters.

❄

THE CARRIAGE LUMBERED slowly over the icy roads leading from Oxfordshire back to London. There could be no complaints about the quality of the carriage. The squabs were fashioned of silk and leather. The newness of the paint and the surprising lack of sound within as it rattled over treacherous roads suggested it had been recently built. The floor was lined with lush carpet, heated bricks laid at her feet for warmth. Venetian blinds covered the windows, allowing in the gloomy light of the winter's afternoon. It was, Adele had to admit, lushly appointed and elegant.

But it was not any carriage in which she traveled. No, indeed. This was her husband's carriage.

Adele was *married*.

Her father was going to have her hide. Her mama would swoon when word reached her in Cornwall, where she had gone to look after her own ailing mother. Her sisters Hannah and Evie would be shocked. And Max? She could only hope he would appreciate the sacrifices she had made to keep him safe and that he would change his ways.

Just as she could only hope Mr. Dominic Winter would prove a good husband.

A hysterical burst of laughter fled her.

There was a limit to her hope, and believing the darkly handsome man across from her could ever be a good husband, the sort she had once wished for herself, was laughable.

"Are you weeping or are you laughing, Duchess?"

Her gaze flitted from the window to settle upon the man she had wed. "Mayhap a combination of both."

"I prefer your laughter to your tears."

His solemn pronouncement took her by surprise. "I would think a man such as yourself takes pleasure in tears."

"The tears of certain others, yes." He cocked his head to the side, a small, almost boyish smile curling his sensual lips. "Your tears? Never."

"And yet you forced me to marry you," she reminded him. "I know what you did, making certain Lady Emilia and Mr. Winter would discover where you had gone at just the right moment to create maximum damage to my reputation."

"I may have paid a servant." He gave an indolent shrug.

"Bribed, you mean."

He truly was a wicked man. Conscienceless, willing to cross any boundary in pursuit of what he wanted. And what he had wanted had been her. What she did not understand yet was why. Adele meant to get to the bottom of the mystery.

Soon.

"Why quibble over a word, Duchess?" His grin deepened.

"Why indeed? A liar is no better than a thief, is he?"

His lips twitched. "Are you calling me a liar or a thief, love?"

There was deceptive calm in his voice, his tone smooth and mellifluous. And yet, there was also an undeniable edge. He was mercurial, Dominic Winter. She could not begin to understand him, and that terrified her. Because she was forever bound to him now.

Still, she refused to allow him to see the effect he had upon her. She could be brave. All her life, she had been the quiet twin, the wallflower. She had proven to herself, however, that when the situation merited her efforts, she was stronger than she had ever known.

She studied him now. "I have no way of knowing if you are either of those things. I scarcely know you at all, Mr. Winter."

His brows snapped into a frown. "Dom."

He could keep all London trembling in fear at the thought of his wrath, but she would not cower. "You forced me to marry you, but you cannot choose what I call you, *Mr. Winter*."

"You will call me Dom," he growled.

"No."

"No?" His voice was steeped in disbelief.

She wondered if anyone ever denied him. Mayhap she would have to be the first. "No, Mr. Winter. I have been thinking about our marriage."

"You have, have you?" There it was again, that barely leashed menace.

"Yes. I do think it would be in the best interest of everyone involved if we were to keep it a secret for a time." Adele bit her lower lip, watching his reaction to her suggestion.

Truly, her initial plan had been to escape him. But he had

thwarted her at every turn. Finally, she had decided there was no other means of saving herself aside from marrying him. At least she had gotten his promise that Max would be safe.

But her husband's response was not what she had been hoping for.

"Never," he vowed, vehement.

Curse him.

"Only think of it, Mr. Winter. We will have time to make our announcement to society. I can return to my father's townhome, and you shall go back to The Devil's Spawn. In time, we can reach a suitable agreement between the two of us."

"Who is it you think you have married, *Mrs. Winter?*"

Mrs. Winter. Good heavens, how strange it sounded.

His tone was a warning, and she knew it. But she was not in the mood to retreat. She was in the mood to fight. Battle was all she had left, because she feared what would become of her and her child. She could not raise a babe in a gaming hell.

"I do not know whom I have married." He was a stranger, an enigma. She was fascinated by him, frightened of him, desperately drawn to him.

He was the wicked seducer every society mother warned her daughters about.

And she had given in to him.

Had given herself to him.

"Allow me to rectify, Duchess." Grasping the straps, he rose to comical height, hunkered over, balancing himself with an ease that belied the state of the wintry roads. He bowed. "Dominic Winter. Pleased to make your acquaintance."

With that pronouncement, he tipped the brim of an imaginary hat and settled himself once more on the expensive squabs opposite her. *Heavens take the man.* That had been…charming. Her lips wanted to curve into a smile.

She bit her lip again, hard, to keep that unwanted expression at bay. "I am more than aware of your name. You are being obtuse to irritate me."

He grinned. "Is it working?"

Once more, her lips twitched. He had not been wrong when he had warned her she had made a bargain with the devil. Only the devil himself could be so smooth, so charismatic, so commanding and dangerous all at once.

"You are fortunate you did not strike your head on the roof of the carriage with your antics," she told him instead of admitting anything.

"I never take risks unless I know they are in my favor." His grin changed, deepening into a true smile.

The corners of his eyes wrinkled. Her breath caught.

Blessed angels, when he smiled, truly smiled, he was...the most beautiful man she had ever seen.

His words finally settled into the cracks he had created in her ability to concentrate. *I never take risks unless I know they are in my favor.*

Telling, that statement.

"Was marrying me a risk in your favor?" she asked him, wondering again at the reason for his abrupt desire to marry her.

He had not wanted to marry her when he had believed her a mere mistress. Was it because she was the daughter of a duke? And yet, he dismissed society and curled his lip at his own half brother.

"Marrying you was an excellent decision," he countered softly, an appreciative light entering his intense stare. "Aside from your impertinence, I have no regrets."

He was doing it again. Charming her.

Blast him.

"I am gratified you do not have regrets, some two hours

after our nuptials, Mr. Winter." She kept her voice carefully cool.

Colder than the January wind outside, howling and buffeting the carriage. The journey to London was not overly long, thankfully. However, with the unusual cold and the bouts of snow they had been suffering, travel was certainly not ideal.

"You are *almost* the most stubborn woman I have ever known," he told her.

She could not be certain if this announcement was an insult or a compliment.

But she did know a sudden pang of jealousy at the notion of him consorting with any other women. Foolish, she knew. Burning in her breast like a hot coal, nonetheless.

"Who *is* the most stubborn woman you have ever known?" she could not resist asking, though she feared the answer.

"My sister." He chuckled. "When you meet Genevieve, you will understand."

Ah yes, there it was again. The specter of his family. A reminder of just how little she truly knew about the man she had just married. "How many siblings do you have, Mr. Winter?"

"Eleven in all that I am aware of. I would not be surprised if another half dozen rattled loose at some point. Old Papa Winter liked to dip his quill into any inkwell he could find."

Her cheeks flushed at her husband's plain speech, and she decided to ignore that particular statement. "How many brothers and sisters do you have, aside from the other Winters?"

"The respectable Winters, you mean?" His tone was grim. "Amongst the disreputable bastards, there is one sister, Genevieve. Then there is Devil, Demon, Blade, and Gavin."

The name Devil brought with it memories of the hulking man who had escorted her to Dominic's office that first night. "Do you have two acquaintances named Devil, or is the ferocious, scowling beast skulking about The Devil's Spawn your brother?"

"I will have to tell him you think him a beast. He will be pleased."

"But he *is* your brother, is he not?"

Now that she thought about it, the two men shared similarly massive, muscular builds. Both were tall, with dark hair. Both menacing.

"He is my half brother. Our mothers were Covent Garden doxies. Apparently Papa Winter had a certain preference. Young, pretty, and desperate."

"Where are your mothers now?"

His jaw tightened. "Gone."

She could not be certain if the glimmer in his dark eyes was grief or something else, but she felt the need to offer her sympathy. Life in the streets of London could not have been easy. "I am sorry."

"I do not require your pity, Duchess. Our mothers sold us to one of their patrons for a bit of coin. Neither Devil nor I have mourned their passing."

"Sold you?" Adele had never heard of such a thing, the selling of children. Surely it could not mean what she feared?

"To a man who wanted to…" He stopped, shaking his head. "It matters not. Devil saved us both before it went too far."

She wanted to know more. Indeed, Adele was startled to realize she wanted to know everything there was to know about him. He intrigued her. He terrified her. He…made her feel things she had never felt before.

He was also the father of her child.

A child whose existence she had yet to inform him of.

Adele was going to tell him, she decided. But then, the carriage rolled to a stop outside a coaching inn, and he threw open the door to the conveyance as if he could not wait a moment longer to remove himself from it.

An icy wall of winter's wind hit her.

Fitting.

She held her tongue and followed her new husband into the inn.

Chapter Ten

HIS WIFE WAS asleep.
Floating hell.

His first evening as a married man was not progressing as Dom had hoped it would when he had gone to the public rooms for ale. He had been doing his damnedest to be considerate. A new state for him, it was certain. She had suggested she needed some time to attend to private matters.

One pint had turned into another. Then another.

Until he had decided it would be prudent to return to his bride.

To his *sleeping* bride.

Dom had spent every second since he had bedded her the first time plotting and dreaming what it would be like to have her again. His need for her had only grown more pronounced, the more time he spent in her presence. The ale in the public rooms had been his attempt at being a gentleman.

It had been either get a bit tap-hackled in an effort to quell his raging cockstand or fall upon her like a starving beggar who had been deprived of sustenance for long enough to make him go mad. He had also made certain his pickpocket did not go about separating any of the guests at the inn from their purses.

Davy, as Dom had discovered the lad's name was, had bedded down in the stables with his coachman for the night, each of them with a warm mug of cider and the rich meat pies of the proprietress filling their bellies. Dom was not entirely certain the lad's word was good, but he fully intended to make certain the little thief had complied by the light of the morning.

Still, the hour was early, and he had not expected Lady Adele to be in blissful slumber when he returned to their rooms. At least she had thought to lock the door. Her trusting nature did not apparently extend to fellow travelers, thank Christ.

With a sigh, Dom stalked toward the hearth where the fire had already gone low. The air had a pronounced nip to it, and he could not abide by cold. Mayhap it was the result of living on the streets for so much of his youth. There was nothing worse than a London winter with no roof and scarcely any food.

He stoked the fire, then stood before it, allowing the flames to warm him. Wondering what he would do. He ought to wake her and claim her. Strip her out of her travel weeds and sink inside her where he belonged. Fuck her until the sun rose.

The Dominic Winter he had always believed himself to be would have done so, he was sure of it. He would have had no quarter for a fancy duke's daughter who had the effrontery to fall asleep on their wedding night. But ever since Lady Adele Saltisford had entered his life, he had gone despicably soft.

Not his prick, he thought grimly. That part of his anatomy had failed to change. He wanted her more than he had ever desired another woman.

But his mind, his resolve, his ruthlessness—those traits which had kept him in power amidst the bloodthirsty, grasping monsters of the rookeries—seemed to have been affected. What the devil was this sudden affliction? Did it have a name?

Grimly, he turned and stalked back toward the bed where Adele lay sleeping. Her lovely face was relaxed, her lips parted. She had not shed anything save her bonnet, gloves, and pelisse. And nor had she bothered to draw down the counterpane or remove her boots.

In the low, flickering light, she looked every bit the angel he had once believed her. She also looked bloody uncomfortable. Not that he cared, of course.

He was Dominic Winter. He cared for his siblings who shared his blood. He worried over his empire, his money, his power. He most certainly did not fret over a spoiled daughter to a duke who had lied to him, run from him, and then fallen asleep before he could enjoy his wedding night, curse it.

Curse her.

He was moving toward her before he realized what he was doing, his damned legs possessing a mind of their own. Dom stopped at the foot of the bed. Her boots were as fine as she was, fashioned of white cotton and kid, laced with satin, and highly impractical.

He untied the knot on her right boot first, then the left. He slid them off to reveal small, dainty feet encased in stockings. Never in his life had the sight of a woman's toes affected him. Hell, he had been hard pressed to notice they even possessed them.

Until now.

Her toes were cold. The realization bothered him. Dom set about warming them in his hands. She shifted on the bed, making a deep, throaty sound of satisfaction that went directly to his cock. Because all the sense he had once possessed had fled him utterly, he began rubbing her feet, using his thumbs on her arches. Just to hear more of her satisfied purrs, he told himself. Not because he wanted to tend to her.

His gaze traveled the length of her. She lay on her side, her arms cradling her midriff. So trusting, so serene. Dipped in sunshine, she was. And foolish. Did she not know what manner of man she had married, to trust him implicitly enough that she fell asleep before he returned to their shared rooms and bed?

It occurred to him then that neither of them had eaten. Surely she must be hungry. He flicked the opposite end of the counterpane over her, making certain it was tucked all around her, before he tried to wake her.

"Duchess?" Gently, he brushed a dark tendril of hair that had fallen over her face from her cheek. "Time to wake, love."

Her eyes did not open. Instead, she nuzzled her cheek into his palm in the fashion of a satisfied cat. "Mmm."

Damn her. This woman excelled at torture. He wanted her so desperately, he could scarcely breathe, and she was sleeping like a babe.

He gave her shoulder a light shake next. "Adele, wake up."

Her eyes flew open at last, and she jolted, as if he had just hauled her from somewhere pleasant.

She blinked at him. "Dom?"

Finally, he had his way. She had called him Dom. The victory was a hollow one, however. She remained half in the grip of slumber. He was still stroking her cheek. Disgusted with himself, he withdrew his touch.

"Do you intend to sleep all evening, Duchess? I, for one, would like to have my supper." His voice was curt, possessing the stinging lash of a whip, and he knew it.

Her brow furrowed. "Forgive me. I did not intend to fall asleep. I have been so tired since I have…been traveling. I had no wish to displease you."

He frowned down at her, feeling like an arse. The pause

in her words had not slipped past him. He was a man who studied the expressions, eyes, and words of everyone around him at all times. His life and his position depended upon it.

"You have been so tired since you have been what, Duchess?" he probed, suspicious.

If she meant to betray him, if she had been somehow colluding against him, he would show her no mercy. He needed her as his wife, but he was not afraid to do what he must.

"Since I have been traveling, as I said," she repeated, her gaze flitting from his as she sat up. "Long carriage rides do not agree with me, I am afraid. They make me dreadfully weary."

She was lying.

Dom knew it.

Why? And what was she seeking to hide from him? He would have to get to the heart of the matter later.

"The fare here is not what you are accustomed to, but my lad and coachman tell me the meat pies are quite good." He extended his hand to her. "If you wish it, I will have a tray of them sent up with some wine and ale."

Her small, elegant hand settled in his big, rough one. "That sounds lovely, Dom."

She had called him by his given name again. His fingers tightened on hers and he pulled her to her feet in one effortless gesture. There was much he needed to learn about this wife of his.

But first, dinner.

❄

DINNER WAS AN unusually intimate affair compared to the multiple courses served by dozens of liveried servants Adele was accustomed to. Wine, fresh bread and butter, and a meat pie on humble crockery, and yet there was something about the simplicity that pleased her. She was seated opposite her husband at a scarred table, the firelight and a lone brace of candles their sole illumination.

Her stomach rumbled noisily at the scent on the air—meat and crust, buttery and rich. She pressed a hand to her midriff, all too aware of the gentle swell beneath her gown. Soon enough, she would have to see her stays altered, her gowns let out. Or perhaps commission a new wardrobe that would accommodate her changing form…

Oh, who was she fooling? That is what she would have done as the wife of a lord. What did the wife of a London crime lord do?

"You are hungry, Duchess. Eat."

Her husband's baritone rumbled through the silence that had fallen between them, and she wished she did not like it quite as much as she did.

She *was* hungry. However, she wanted to speak with him first, to find her footing on this slippery, unfamiliar ground she trod. "You make a habit of feeding me, it seems."

"You make a habit of needing to be fed."

His concern for her wellbeing took her by surprise. It was not what she would have expected from the hardened, merciless man she supposed him. But his actions this evening took her back to the man she had met almost three months ago at The Devil's Spawn.

He had been formidable, yes. Terrifying also. But then, he had been the man who had insisted they dine before following through with their bargain. He had kissed her with such tenderness. He had touched her as if she were fashioned of the finest Sèvres.

And this evening, when she had fallen into an exhausted sleep, she had risen to find he had removed her boots and tucked the bedclothes around her. Adele's lady's maid had not made the journey to Oxfordshire from London, and she had been using first her sister's lady's maid for the duration of the house party, then sharing with her obliging hostess after Hannah and Evie had departed.

Still, she hesitated to eat. She had before her a rare opportunity with Dominic Winter, and she meant to seize it.

"I am wearing the straps today, indeed," she said, remembering what he had said to Devereaux Winter and thinking to impress him with her use of cant.

But her husband gave her a puzzled frown instead. "Wearing the straps, Duchess? Is that some sort of lady's undergarment?"

"Yes, wearing the straps," she said agreeably. "That is what you said to Mr. Winter to indicate you were hungry, is it not?"

A short burst of laughter fled him.

Drat. Apparently, it was not. How had she mucked it up? She had been so certain…

Adele's cheeks went hot.

"Near enough, Duchess. Wearing the *bands* is what you want." He grinned. "I applaud the attempt. We'll have you speaking flash in no time."

His words seemed somewhat ominous to her.

"We?"

He broke off a hunk of bread and slathered it with butter. "My brothers and sister. They all live in the hell with me, and so shall you."

He expected her to live in a gaming hell, just as she had feared. Perhaps he would change his mind when he realized there would be a child. One could only hope.

"You do not consider the other Winters family?" she queried, curious.

The enmity between Devereaux Winter and her husband had been plain to see, and yet the family had hosted him. He had come to Abingdon Hall. She knew from conversations with them following Dominic's surprise arrival that the Winter sisters had not been aware of their shared parentage, but Mr. Winter had been.

"No," he clipped. "I do not."

"Why not?"

His frown deepened. "I thought you were wearing the straps, Duchess."

"The bands," she corrected, gamely. "And you did not answer my question, Mr. Winter."

"Back to Mr. Winter, am I? Must mean I've got you in a dudgeon." He took a bite of his bread, chewing slowly, deliberately.

Was it her imagination, or did Dominic Winter make the uninteresting act of eating bread erotic?

"If you answer my questions with other questions, I will call you Mr. Winter," she said simply. "I am attempting to become better acquainted with my husband."

"That's what the bed is for, love." He winked.

Heat flared in her cheeks once more. "I did not mean to suggest in that fashion, sir."

"Fuck me, you're beautiful when you flush."

Such vulgar praise from any other gentleman in the world would have had no effect upon Adele save insult. She would have boxed his ears.

But when Dominic Winter told her she was beautiful, it did strange things to her insides. She forgot to be offended. Indeed, she rather liked the sound of that naughty word on his lips, his facile tongue.

"You still have yet to answer my question," she managed.

"Like a bloody dog with a bone, you are." He sighed, then

took a sip of his ale, his dark gaze never straying from her as he made her wait. "Fine, Duchess. You win. The bastard Winters are my family. Devereaux Winter can stuff his papa's money and his society connections up his—"

"Mr. Winter," she interrupted, before he could say something else that was regrettable.

"Nose," he finished, his grin returning. "Here is the way of it, love. Devereaux Winter discovered the existence of us bastards when old Papa Winter cocked up his toes. I knew about Devil and Blade, but Demon, Gavin, and Genevieve were a surprise to me. The first thing I did after he gave me the news was to tell him to sod off and the second thing I did was to find all my siblings."

"You brought all the bastard Winters together."

He glowered at her. "Do not be thinking me a saint, Duchess. If any one of them had proved a liability to me, Devil, and Blade, we would have cut ties the way I did with Devereaux Winter."

Somehow, she did not believe him. Adele suspected his hatred of Devereaux Winter had everything to do with his pride. The little she had come to know of Dominic thus far suggested he would not have reacted kindly to Devereaux Winter's offer of money. Particularly since Devereaux Winter was a legitimate heir and Dominic had been raised in the slums by a mother who had *sold* him for purposes she refused to contemplate.

"I do not think you are as hardhearted as you would have me believe." Carefully, she tucked into her meat pie.

The first bite was an explosion of decadent, hearty flavors on her tongue. She had eaten meals prepared by some of the finest chefs in the realm, and yet the rich, buttery crust and well-seasoned meat and vegetables in her mouth could compete with ease.

She could not quite stifle her moan of enjoyment, unladylike though it was. And who was there to judge her, anyway? She was sharing a table with an East End rogue who had just uttered some of the foulest language imaginable to her.

Her husband muttered something that sounded like an epithet which was even viler and took a lengthy draught of ale. She watched in fascination as his pronounced Adam's apple bobbed with each sip.

He had removed his cravat at some point, and she approved of his decision. His throat was ridiculously handsome. She was certain she had never been so riveted by the sight of a man's neck before.

"If any man is within twenty paces of you when you eat a meat pie, I'll gut him like a fish," he proclaimed, setting his tankard on the table with so much force, the crockery rattled and jumped.

Adele swallowed the heaven on her tongue at last. "What is the matter with the manner in which I eat meat pie?"

"You are dipped in sunshine, aren't you, Duchess?" He shook his head. "Suffice it to say watching you eat a meat pie will only make a man think of you putting something else between your pretty, pink lips."

Oh.

She understood what he meant now. Strangely, the notion of putting his *something else* between her lips was not at all unwelcome. Indeed, she was curious. He had used his tongue upon her, and the effect had been quite wondrous.

Good heavens, what was happening to her? She had been married to this man for the mere span of a day and already, he had thoroughly corrupted her.

Her ears felt as if they had been doused in flame. "I shall endeavor to always eat alone, Mr. Winter."

"I hope you will eat with me. Often."

Was that an invitation?

From Dominic Winter?

"I thought you were angry with me for misleading you." She took another bite of her dinner and barely suppressed a second moan.

"For *lying* to me, Duchess. And yes, I still am. But that does not mean a man cannot enjoy his lady wife." He raised a brow, the blatant sensuality burning in his gaze leaving no doubt as to his meaning.

"Why did you marry me?" she could not help but to ask again. "You never did explain yourself. And before you repeat your nonsensical claim you wished to marry a duke's daughter to compete with Deveraux Winter, be advised that I do not believe a word of it. There is another reason entirely."

It stood to reason there was something for him to gain, but Adele could not fathom what he hoped to have. There was her dowry, yes, but if her father did not approve of their union—which she knew without a doubt he would not—she would not get a penny. There was also the matter of Dominic Winter's wealth. A man in need of funds did not turn down an inheritance for the sake of his pride.

"I wanted to marry you because ever since you first started making trouble for me at The Devil's Spawn, I have been able to think of little else," he told her, his tone smooth.

So smooth she did not believe him.

"You mean to say you have been so thoroughly distracted by thoughts of me, Mr. Winter, that the only solution to your problem was forcing me into a marriage I did not want and using my brother as the leverage you required?" she repeated, allowing her disbelief to bleed through her tone.

He shrugged. "Sounds about right."

Her eyes narrowed. "And now which one of us is the liar?"

He grinned. "I know which one of us I trust and which one of us I don't."

Fair enough, but two could play at that game.

"As do I. But I have never given you cause to doubt me, Mr. Winter."

"Have *I* given *you* cause to doubt me, Duchess? Tell me how."

They stared at each other, at a stalemate.

"You have made me marry you," she pointed out.

"I did not hear you offer any arguments to the clergyman," he countered.

"Because you threatened my brother."

"I hate to be the bearer of ill tidings, Duchess, but I was never the one responsible for the beating old Sundenbury took."

This was news to her. She sat up straighter in her seat. "One of your men, then."

"Not my men either. Your brother has been playing too deep with the wrong East End scoundrels, love, and now they want what is owed them or his blood."

Speaking of scoundrels.

Shock washed over her. "Do you mean to say you were not responsible for what happened to Max?"

"Neither I nor my men." He took another lengthy draught of his ale. "Bad business to go about beating the quality. Words gets round. I have other methods of persuasion at my disposal when collecting what is owed me."

He had deceived her. Misled her. And to what end? To make her his wife? Anger and outrage rose within her, battling for supremacy.

She was beginning to realize the man she had married was more Machiavellian than she had initially supposed. "Such as cozening ladies into marrying you?"

"Not all ladies, Duchess. Only one."

There was a spark in his gaze that settled deep within her, lighting an answering flame in spite of her every attempt to ignore it and tamp down the unwanted way he made her feel. "I suppose I must be grateful for small mercies."

"Excellent notion, love. Now eat your supper before it goes cold."

She would have argued, but her stomach chose that moment to growl once more with the reminder that she was truly famished. Adele forked up another bite of meat pie and wondered how she was going to navigate the treacherous path ahead.

A path that had nothing to do with ice- and snow-laden roads bound for London and everything to do with navigating her relationship with the dangerous man she had married.

Chapter Eleven

DOM COULD NOT sleep.

Likely because his mind was still addled from the suspected poison brother dearest had slipped into his wassail, he had decided to play the gentleman.

That was the only reason he had not immediately kissed his wife senseless following dinner, then stripped her out of her gown and stockings and made love to her all night long. Certainly, it had nothing to do with the budding sensation in his chest, which he refused to believe was tenderness.

He had not turned his back to give her modesty while she slipped beneath the thick blankets because she had seemed so drowsy following their meal. Nor had he lowered the lights and banked the fire before climbing into the opposite side of the bed in his breeches and shirt because he was feeling guilty for manipulating her into wedding him.

Because Dominic Winter was not merciful. Nor was he kind. Or considerate. And above all, he did not care for anyone outside the immediate circle of his sister and brothers. He could not afford to be anything other than the man he was, fashioned of cold, lead, and steel.

One brunette duke's daughter with the lushest lips he had ever kissed would not change him. This he vowed as he shifted in the bed, attempting to find a comfortable position and willing his rigid cock to wilt. She was a means to an end.

Damn it, how was he going to get any rest tonight knowing she was sharing the same bed, within arm's reach? Knowing the seductive warmth beneath the bedclothes belonged to her?

On a sigh, he attempted to adjust himself. But that only made the need pulsing through him even more pronounced. And worse, because he wanted her to be the one touching him. He wanted to pin her to the bed and make love to her until the sun rose.

"Floating hell," he grumbled into the darkness of the night.

"Is something amiss?"

Her husky question startled him. From the soft, even breaths she had been taking, he had been convinced she was asleep.

"Go to sleep, Duchess."

"Do you have an aversion to questions, Mr. Winter?"

Fancy words from the fancy lady he had married. He clenched his jaw. That ought to have made his cockstand die a hasty death, the reminder she was of the quality and yet another question, coupled with her insistence on calling him *Mr. Winter*.

If anything, it only made him harder. As did the knowledge she was awake.

"Do you have an aversion to calling me Dom?" he countered softly.

Part of him knew he should just flop on his belly and go the hell to sleep. Part of him could not resist her. She was dangerous, this woman. He wanted her far too much.

Far more than he should.

Far more than was safe.

"Why do you have a predilection for answering one question with another?" came her voice through the inkiness of the cool night.

Soft and seductive, that dulcet tone. It did things to him. Made him long for things he could never have. Happiness. Love. Arms to hold him, a heart which could be his.

But no. These were the foolish longings of the lad he had once been. Life had taught him those fantasies belonged in the ashes of a fire rather than meandering through his restless mind.

He turned his thoughts back to the question she had asked. "Mayhap you ask questions I have no wish to answer, Duchess."

"We can spend all evening turning in circles, or you can give me what I want."

Her words curled around him, like a siren's song. Luring him to the death. His entire body was a conflagration, on fire with want. Desire for her overwhelmed him. Consumed him.

He rolled to his side so he faced her instead of the wall. "And what is it you want?"

Her swift inhalation cut through the silence. "I did not mean that the way it sounded."

Too tempting, his wife. He envisioned her cheeks, emblazoned with pretty color. Imagined her curves, hidden by nothing save the thin night rail he had managed a glimpse of before politely turning his back. It had been too long since he'd had a woman. The last time had been with her. Because ever since she had found her way into his life and his bed, she was the only woman who owned his thoughts. The only woman he wanted.

Curse her.

"How did you mean it then, Duchess?"

"Would you cease calling me that?"

She was right. Angel had suited her better. Until she had disappeared and he had uncovered her deception.

"What would you have me call you instead?"

"My sisters call me Addie," she ventured.

He growled. "If you have yet to notice, I am hardly your sister."

"I am more than aware of that."

He did not miss the breathlessness in her tone. The urge to touch her was sudden and insistent. So he did. Slowly, tentatively. He was aiming for her shoulder. What his fingers sank into instead was the lush, silken skeins of her hair.

Fucking hell, she must have pulled the pins from it and let down her hair after he had blown out the candles. He had to tamp down a groan. He was an ardent admirer of all aspects of Lady Adele's beauty, but her hair was utterly bloody gorgeous. He had fantasized about running his fingers through it, about spreading the dark curls over his pillow. About burying his face in the fragrant mass and inhaling, of holding a handful as he buried himself deep inside her beautiful body.

"I love your hair."

The admission rumbled from him before he could banish it. Entirely unwanted. Ridiculous, in fact. He was not the sort of man who issued such compliments. Who worried about a woman's hair. Who gently stroked it in the darkness, following its cascade over her pillow.

Damn it, yes he was. Because he was doing all that now. How much ale had he consumed? Perhaps it was the combination of brother dearest's poisoned wine and the ale which had done him in.

"You can call me Adele if you like," she whispered.

"Adele." He found the sweet warmth of her cheek then, cupping it. "May I kiss you?"

Someone ought to beat him. If the Suttons could see him now—the mighty Dominic Winter, asking his wife's permission to kiss her—they would laugh first and pull out a shiv and bury it between his ribs next.

But none of that mattered because one word flitted to him, and all other thoughts fled his mind.

"Yes."

Thank Christ. He slid himself nearer, so their bodies were aligned. Through the shadows, he found her lips. She opened for him on a sigh. He wasted no time in deepening the kiss, his tongue slipping past the seam of her mouth to tangle with hers. She tasted sweet and rich. Hunger roared through him. He told himself to proceed slowly, to avoid overwhelming her.

But he had been starving for her ever since he had first laid eyes on her. Having her once had not sated him. It had only made him desire her more. She was an infection, a fever in his blood. He was helpless to do anything but surrender.

Her arms twined around his neck and she sidled nearer, until they were pressed fully against each other, nothing but the barrier of cloth between them. She kissed him back with a fierceness that took him by surprise.

Adele's response undid him.

Any attempts at restraint were impossible as her fingernails raked over his shoulders, scoring his flesh through the thin fabric of his shirt. He sucked on her lower lip, then trailed a path of kisses along her jaw. Lower. Down the softness of her throat. He kissed her ear, nibbled the cord of her neck. She smelled like spring and sunshine and everything that was good.

He wanted to keep her in his arms forever.

Dom rolled her to her back and settled between her thighs, leveraging himself on his forearms to keep from crushing her beneath the weight of his body. Her night rail did nothing to hide the fullness of her breasts or the hardness of her nipples. He knew instinctively that if he skimmed a hand up her inner thigh to her center, he would find her wet and ready for him.

But their garments were an encumbrance he was determined to shed this time around. When he made love to her tonight, now that she was his wife, he wanted no barriers between them. He wanted only her skin on his. He wanted her burning into him, her curves searing his flesh, marked forever upon him.

"I want you, Adele," he murmured against her cloth-covered breast.

His mouth discovered her nipple, and he sucked.

She moaned, arching up to meet him, her response more pronounced than he had recalled. Dom moved to the other breast, suckling that one as well. Her fingers traveled to his hair, caressing a path of fire over his scalp.

The way she touched him, so tenderly, made him wild.

"Please," she said.

He knew what she wanted. Understood the raw need underscoring her sweet voice. She was every bit as desperate for their joining as he was. He rose on his knees, and tore his shirt over his head. The scars that marred his flesh could not shock her beneath the cloak of darkness.

But then her hands were on him, curious and tentative at first, sweeping up his abdomen. Arrows of pure fire shot through him. Her fingertips were softer than silk. As pleasurable as he found her touch upon his bare skin, however, he was not ready for her to feel the ugly puckers and slashes, remnants and reminders of his past. Too ugly for this night, this woman.

He caught her hands in his and lifted them to his lips. "Patience, love."

"Do you not like it when I touch you?"

Her hesitant query cut through him. How did she sense so much, know so much?

"I have scars," he shocked himself by revealing. "They are not fit for a lady's touch."

In the darkness, he could discern her silhouette as she rose to a sitting position. She tugged her hands from his. "I do not care if you have scars. I want to feel you, to know you. If you will allow it."

She was asking his permission. He ought to tell her no. Ought to tug her night rail over her head, toss it to the floor, and make her his. Yet, the part of him he could not begin to understand longed for that touch. Desperately. He placed her hands on his chest.

"Do your worst, Duchess," he rasped.

"Adele." Her fingertips moved tentatively. "Call me Adele, and I shall call you Dom."

The barriers he needed between them were gone. The literal, the figurative. Her touch glided over him, investigating the slash marks, the puckered wound on his shoulder from the pistol ball that had grazed him in a street fight.

"Adele," he repeated, allowing her this victory as her name emerged from him, half groan and half croak.

"Your scars do not frighten me." She completely undid him by pressing her mouth over the old, healed wounds. She kissed him everywhere, missing not a bare expanse of skin.

And he remained still beneath the tender onslaught of her ministrations. Allowing her to touch and kiss him wherever she would. He told himself he was enabling her this liberty because the fading glow of the firelight left him blanketed in enough shadows to obscure the hideousness of his scars from her. But deep within, he knew it for a lie.

It was because she was Adele.

Because she was dipped in sunlight, and he wanted to steal some of that brightness for his own. He wanted to savor it, to savor *her*, forever.

When she reached the jagged scar on his abdomen that ended beneath his breeches, just over his hip, she paused. "What happened to you, Dom? Who hurt you like this?"

The anguish in her voice should have revolted him. Instead, it seeped inside him, filling all the cracks and fissures like warm honey.

"Enemies. Do not fret over me, love. These wounds are long since healed."

Her lips traced the scar. "Has anyone tried to hurt you recently?"

What was this? Concern for him?

More honey, filling in the places he had believed no longer existed. More sweetness he should not long for.

"I have Devil and Blade to protect me, along with dozens of others. You need not worry for me." He could not wait another moment to get her naked. His hands grasped the diaphanous fabric of her night rail. "I want this off you."

She helped him, hauling the gown over her head without a single hesitation. Then her fingers settled on the fastening of his breeches. Getting himself free of them took far more time than he preferred, and in the end, he had to tear them from his limbs. If he'd had an inkling that his wife wanted him every bit as much as he wanted her before they had settled into bed for the night, he damn well would have divested himself of every bleeding stitch.

At last, the breeches were gone, and there were no barriers left between them. Dom took her lips, kissing her as he guided her back to the bed linens. Her arms went around him like a benediction. It almost shamed him, how easily she welcomed him, how trusting she was. He did not deserve this woman.

But he was going to keep her anyway.

Dom dragged his lips from hers, pressing his mouth to her velvety skin. She was smooth and sleek. And warm. So bloody warm. He kissed to the peaks of her breasts, sucking hard on her nipples as his fingers dipped between her legs. Responsive, too.

She let out a breathy moan as he parted her folds to find her slick and swollen, ready for him. He circled her pearl, stroking her with quick, firm movements that had her body jerking from the bed to meet him.

Although he was desperate to be inside her, nothing could keep him from kissing lower, down the curve of her belly. All the way to her mound. He teased her slick lips with his thumb, opening her. The shadows did nothing to deter his enjoyment. He knew how pink and glistening she was.

He licked her.

As before, she tasted musky and delicious. And the husky mewl of pleasure that emerged from her—*fuck*, it made Dom wild. Wilder than he already was. He sank a finger inside her sheath. She was tight, gripping him with her heat. It was like coming home.

A reunion he had been awaiting three long months.

Yes, said the wicked voice inside him. *More*.

He drew her bud into his mouth, devouring her.

Mine, said the voice.

"Dom," keened his wife.

He nipped her, softly, tenderly. Enough to incite pleasure rather than pain. He would not hurt this woman for the world. He, Dominic Winter, who had bloodied his fists in the street, who had fought with blade and bullet, who had never given a damn about anyone save his sister and brothers, would give his life for her.

She was his family now. Cleaved to him. Joined with him. *His*.

He licked down her seam, replacing his finger with his tongue. Diving deep into her slippery channel. Her hips bucked. As he worked her pearl and thrust his tongue into her, she came, shuddering beneath him, the most decadent sounds of surrender he'd ever heard shattering the night.

He could not wait another moment.

He was upon her in an instant, rigid cock in hand, guiding himself to her center.

"Tell me what you want," he growled, needing her affirmation.

They were about to consummate their union. Later, he would worry about what was to come. How a duke's daughter could exist in his world, especially after she discovered the truth. Now, all he knew was that he needed her.

Needed her more than his next breath.

"I want you, Dom," she whispered.

He moved. One quick thrust, and he was inside her. She tightened on him, drawing him deeper into her silken warmth. She was as tight as he remembered, and the constriction of her cunny on his cock sent sparks through him. His ballocks tightened.

Sealing their mouths once more, he kissed her as he rocked inside her. Their tongues tangled, the taste of her lacing their frantic meeting of lips. Though he tried to control himself, she felt too good around him, bathing him in the wetness of her spend. His thrusts were faster. More frenzied.

But she did not mind. If anything, his bewitching wife spurred him on, wrapping her leg around his waist, using a foot planted on the mattress to meet his driving rhythm. He was already reaching the end of his limit, and far faster than he had intended, when she clenched on him, coming all over his cock.

He broke their kiss and threw back his head, pumping into her a few more times before he lost all semblance of control. There was a roaring in his ears, flames licking up his spine, as he poured himself into his wife, filling her with his seed.

Mindless, boneless, and spent, he collapsed to the bed at her side. His last coherent thought was that mayhap she would have his child. The notion did not terrify him nearly as much as it ought. For the second time in his life, Dominic Winter fell into a deep, dreamless sleep next to the woman in his bed.

❄

ADELE WOKE TO the familiar chill of a winter's morning, the fire having died sometime during the night. She had slept so soundly. She stretched beneath the covers, feeling sated and sore in strange places. As her eyes fluttered open to meet the light pouring through the gaps in the window dressing, she expected to find herself in the gold bedchamber at Abingdon Hall, where she had spent the last few weeks.

The sight greeting her instead was that of a decidedly uninspiring room. Spare and well-used, outfitted with a fireplace and a scarred table with two chairs, along with a chaise longue and a worn carpet, this room and its somewhat dingy walls bore no comparison to the intricate plasterwork and luxurious appointments of her former lodgings.

Remembrance washed over her.

The room was not the only difference, waking up this morning. There was a big, masculine body in the bed with her, an arm slung about her waist, hot breath fanning her nape, a long leg tangled with hers. Dominic Winter was in the bed with her.

Her husband.

The memory of the night before, his tenderness and the pleasure he had wrung from her body once more, filled her with warmth despite the cold of the chamber. He was a complicated man, but she felt certain, after last night, there was hope for them. He had allowed her to know a side of him she suspected he did not readily share.

His scars were many and vicious, some more so than others. His poor body had been ravaged by wounds. And yet, he had allowed her to touch him. He had held still for her shocked examination.

At her side, he made a low, sleepy sound.

She turned toward him, wanting to see how he looked in slumber. So often, he was harsh and forbidding. A man feared by many. A man who had suffered much, she suspected.

Protectiveness for him surged. His handsome countenance was soft, almost boyish. His dark hair was a charming slash falling over his brow, his full, sensual lips parted. A thin stubble of whiskers darkened his unshaven jaw.

Adele could not contain the urge to feel its prickle upon her palm.

Tentatively, she reached for him. But she had scarcely run her hand along the prominent slant when a manacle grip clamped on her wrist and she found herself suddenly rolled to her back, a heavy weight pinning her body to the mattress.

Her arms were wrenched over her head, held to the bed, and the face hovering over hers did not resemble the man she had been quietly admiring at all. His lip curled in a snarl, his eyes flashed with darkness, and his entire body seemed poised to strike.

Terror leapt into her throat, her heart pounding in her breast. "Dom!"

He blinked. The fight fled him. His body relaxed, his expression shifting. Softening once more, this time with regret rather than boyish charm. "Adele? Fuck, I am so sorry, love. Have I done you injury?"

As he asked the question, he released her wrists and removed his body from hers. Her wrists throbbed with the sudden force he had shown, and his unexpected response still had her pulse racing, but she was otherwise unaffected.

What had happened in Dominic Winter's life to make him suspect someone was attempting to harm him in his sleep?

"I am fine," she told him, rubbing her wrists, frowning. "But what of you, Dom? Did you think I was going to harm you?"

"Not you." He gritted a low curse, passing his hand over his face. "Floating hell, love. I am sorry. I ought to have slept on the floor."

"On the floor? Why?"

He rose from the bed without offering a response, stalking away from her. Adele was briefly shocked by the sight of him, tall, nude, commanding. His body was well-muscled. She had never seen a naked man. But her surprise was not just in his nudity, which did not appear to concern him at all.

Rather, it was in the scars marring his back and legs. Long, diagonal scars marked his back in a pattern. On his thighs and calves, a map of slashes covered him.

She gasped.

"Fuck," he growled, bending down to retrieve his discarded breeches from the threadbare carpets and donning them. "Forgive me. I was so damned upset at nearly harming you that I forgot what a monster I am by the light of day."

"You are not a monster," she hastened to correct him.

But he was already throwing on his shirt, stalking to the far end of the room, putting distance between them. She gathered the counterpane around her for modesty and slipped from the bed, following him, determined not to allow him to create a deeper chasm than that which already existed.

The haste of her movements proved a mistake.

The vile sickness that had been affecting her returned in a flash. Nausea churned. Her belly tightened.

No, she would not retch now.

Do not be ill. Do not be ill, she charged herself.

Adele swallowed. But the bile was rising. A wave of dizziness hit her, heightening the severity of the nausea. She needed a chamber pot.

Now.

Scrambling, she located the unadorned porcelain basin just in time to fall to her knees and cast up her accounts into it. She heaved again and again, eyes watering as she emptied her stomach. Humiliation washed over her as the sickness subsided.

She became aware of a presence at her side. A cool, damp cloth passed over her face.

"Not a monster, am I?"

Her husband's grim voice did nothing to assuage her misery.

Dear God, he thought she had been sick at the sight of his scars? And still, he was on his knees at her side, tending to her. The notion hurt her heart on his behalf.

But before she could respond, another heave swept over her. She hunched over, attempting to keep her hair from the chamber pot's contents. Another wave of wretchedness swamped her. Her body convulsed, but there was nothing left to bring up into the pot.

And still, he was there, passing the cool, calming cloth over her face once more. His hand traveling up and down her spine in steady, comforting strokes. Even when he believed she was having a violent reaction to his body, he was there for her.

Her heart ached.

The time to tell him the truth was now.

Here.

This moment.

She inhaled through her mouth, then exhaled slowly through her nose, willing her turbulent stomach to calm. A few repetitions, and the aggressive grip of nausea relented. She turned toward her husband, who watched her with an expression that was equal parts guarded and concerned.

"I was not ill because of your scars," she told him.

His expression shuttered. "I do not give a damn if you were. I wear my past with pride. Every mark brought me to the place where I am today. If it disgusts you, you would not be the first. Nor shall you be the last."

His callous words had their intended effect upon her. She wanted to rail against him, but she understood it was only his wounded pride speaking and not the man who had been so patient and gentle with her. For all that he was a feared lord of the East End's criminal enterprises, he was also good. He was the man who kissed her with such sweet tenderness, the man who held her in his arms, the man who made her shatter.

The father of her child.

She must not forget that.

"I am with child."

His swift inhalation cut through the stillness following her revelation.

Adele waited for him to speak, but he said nothing. "Dom?"

"You are carrying a babe."

The words, leaving his lips, seemed to be sharp as blades. They cut her to shreds.

"Your babe," she said. "What did you suppose? I gave myself to you in London. You are the only man I have known."

"You are carrying…my child?"

The question left him slowly, as if the mere asking caused

him undue effort. As if his tongue were rusted, when she knew quite well it was not.

She nodded, breathing slowly again herself to stave off a second rush of nausea. "Of course the babe is yours."

His hand was on her arm, then. The grip was not punishing. But neither was it tender. "You have been carrying my babe for three months and you have yet to inform me of it?"

When he summarized it thus, her actions sounded awful. Unpardonable, even. However, he was forgetting one salient fact.

"I never expected to see you again, Dom. You believed me to be a gentleman's mistress. I gave you my innocence in return for my brother's safety. What happened between us was never meant to be more than what it was that night. And yet…"

His nostrils flared, his gaze searching, holding hers. "And yet?"

She swallowed. "And yet you changed me. You made me see a different side of the world I believed I had known."

He raised a brow. "So different you disappeared and ran off to Oxfordshire?"

"I did not run anywhere." She held his gaze, willing him to see, to understand. "I was an unwed lady who suddenly found herself growing ill in the mornings. Who was hungry and tired. It did not take me long to realize what had happened. I may have been an innocent, but I am not entirely ignorant. I knew I was with child, and so I sought some time. The Winter country house party was the perfect opportunity to escape and plan what I would do next."

Every word she had just spoken had been the truth.

Dom stared at her, his expression harsh, unforgiving. His dark eyes seeking, plumbing, probing. "You knew you were carrying my child, and instead of coming to me, you fled to

Devereaux Winter's country house party to make merry with a bevy of worthless, spoiled aristocrats?"

The seething tone of his voice was a warning.

Her knees ached, and her belly surged again, but this time she was determined to keep her nausea at bay. She did not move, did not flinch.

"How should I have come to you?" she asked him. "I had already brought myself near enough to ruin by finding my way to your gaming hell on two separate occasions without my family being the wiser. I could not risk another trip."

"What was your intention, then?" he demanded, jaw rigid, voice harsh. "If what you say is true, you intended to keep my child from me, did you not?"

She scarcely tamped down the urge to flinch away from the sharpness of his words, the bitter accusation. She could not blame him, because he was not far from the mark.

"I had few choices," she told him evenly, daring him to argue. "I was an unwed lady who found herself in a delicate condition. My father would have never accepted your suit, even if you had been willing to marry me."

He sneered. "Not good enough for you, am I, Duchess?"

She was all too aware he had settled back into his familiar, mocking routine. Was it easier for him to keep her at a distance when he called her by some nonsensical sobriquet? Adele wondered.

Still, she would not allow him to intimidate her. "I have married you, have I not, Mr. Winter?"

"Call me Dom, damn it."

"Then call me Adele, curse you."

They stared at each other, once more at an impasse.

Two stubborn people. Two hearts that seemed to beat as one, when the moment was right. She had to believe there was a reason they had come together. That there was a reason for the child they had created.

"I never supposed I would be a father."

His admission was raw and hoarse, taking Adele by surprise.

"Nor did I suppose I would be a mother just yet," she offered softly, an olive branch extended between them.

His hand closed over hers, their fingers entwining. "Were you running from me?"

"I was running from my father," she confessed. "He would have taken the choice from me. I know what happens to unwed ladies. They are sent to the country, and when they have their lying in, the babes are given to other families so the ladies may return without shame. Few ever know the truth, but the child is gone."

"Is that not what you wanted, to abandon the child to strangers so you could carry on with your life?"

She knew the subject must be particularly painful, given that his own mother had abandoned him. And not just left him, but sold him to someone who would have harmed him in a fashion she did not even wish to comprehend.

"Of course that is not what I wanted, else I would have already been gone. I traveled away from my parents, my father especially, so I could make the decision that suited me best. It is also why I remained in Oxfordshire even after my sisters had left. I did not merely wish to be present at the Duke and Duchess of Coventry's nuptials, though I consider the duchess my friend. I intended to find a cottage somewhere, a place where I could raise the babe and never fear being separated from my child."

His jaw clenched anew. "Instead of coming to me?"

"I did not know you then."

"And do you know me now?"

A strange question. One that was difficult to answer. Nigh impossible, in fact.

But she held his gaze. "I do not think you allow anyone to know you, Dominic Winter. Not truly. Not the entire you. But I want to know you. There is so much more to understand. So much you need to explain. I cannot say what would have happened had you not come to me at Abingdon Hall. But what I do know is that you did, and we are here now, in this moment. We have the opportunity to begin again, together. Will you take it?"

A muscle in his jaw ticked. "You should have sought me out instead of disappearing from my life, Duchess."

"I feared your response, and I feared you, the terrible Mr. Dominic Winter."

"Do you fear me now?"

Her answer was easy. She did not hesitate. "No."

He sighed. "A babe."

"Yes."

Their entwined fingers tightened. Something strange happened in her heart. The last of the fight seemed to have drained from him.

"Ours."

"Ours," she echoed, her heart giving an extra thump.

His expression shifted, softening even more than she had ever seen from him before. "I am going to be a father."

The smile curving her lips was instant. Joyous. Right. "Yes, you are."

He kissed her forehead. "And you shall be a mother."

She nodded, rolling her lips inward as a rush of emotion swept over her. Yet another symptom of her condition, along with the sickness of each morning. "Yes."

"You will be the sort of mother every babe deserves, Duchess."

His quiet words filled her with strength. And something else.

Something that felt a whole lot like love.

Chapter Twelve

THE CARRIAGE CAME to a halt in the mews behind The Devil's Spawn not a moment too soon. Smoke was billowing from one of the upper windows and men were pouring from the back doors.

He had returned to mayhem.

Fucking, floating hell.

"Stay right where you are," he ordered Adele.

Her eyes were wide. "I will do nothing of the sort. I will go where you go. If you are in danger—"

"Damn it, Adele, trust me in this. There may be danger within. If there is, I need to know you will remain where you are safe, that no harm will come to you. Do you understand?"

Her expression turned mulish. "No. I refuse to be relegated to the carriage while you go and face whatever is happening within on your own."

He caught her face in his palms and kissed her swiftly before breaking free. "Listen to me. I…care for you, Adele. I need you and the babe to be safe, and there is no safer place for you than here. This is not a problem you can solve, and every moment I stay here arguing with you is a moment in which one of my men or family could die."

She went ashen at the ruthlessness of his words. "Die? Dom, what is happening?"

He would do all he could to protect her and their child.

But he would not lie to her about the seriousness of the situation. He did have enemies. The Suttons would do anything to overthrow his rule and destroy him. She needed to understand.

Shouts reached him, along with gunfire.

"Fuck." He kissed her again. "Promise me you will stay here. The coachman will protect you. He has instructions to move if the risk of staying here is too great."

She nodded, tears glistening in her dark eyes. "Very well. I promise."

Satisfied, he turned from her and tore open the carriage door.

"Dom?"

Heart pounding, he chanced one last glance at her over his shoulder. "What is it, angel?"

"Stay safe and come back to me."

He gave her a jerky nod. "I will."

With that vow, he turned and leapt from the carriage, slamming the door closed. He would try his damnedest to come back to her. But nothing was certain in his world. Promises were broken. Lives were lost. Power and happiness were fleeting.

He shouted further instruction to the coachman, making certain O'Leary would look after Adele and Davy both. Then he raced into the bedlam surrounding The Devil's Spawn.

There was smoke rolling from the lower hall, but men with buckets of water were everywhere, and the chaos it seemed to be from the outside was actually far more organized within.

"Where is Devil?" he shouted above the din. "And what the hell is happening here?"

One of the men, a sloshing pail hefted on his shoulder, stopped. "Mr. Winter 'as returned, lads!"

A chorus of *Mr. Winter*, along with some huzzahs, echoed in the hall.

It was a reminder this was where he belonged. These were his men. Men who were infallibly loyal. Men who depended upon him for the food in their bellies and the roof overhead. He had not realized how much he had missed The Devil's Spawn until he had returned to find it in an uproar.

"Part!"

The familiar growl rose over the din, and the men obeyed, separating for Devil to stalk through their ranks. His brother was sporting an angry-looking wound over his brow—the blade had scarcely missed gouging the eye and costing him his sight.

"What the hell is going on?" Dom demanded.

"The fire is out now. The damage has been controlled. No one was hurt." Three whole sentences. More than Devil typically said in a sennight.

The blood running down Devil's face suggested the opposite of his calm proclamation. But this was Devil talking, and Dom knew he would never show weakness before their men.

"Back to your posts, you lot," Dom ordered the men, needing to speak with his brother alone. "I heard gunshots when I arrived. Are you certain everything is secure? My wife is waiting in the carriage outside."

"Wife?" Devil's look of disgust could not be misconstrued. He had warned Dom against his plan.

"You knew I was going to marry her. It was my reason for going to Oxfordshire. Now tell me what the hell is going on. This place is bloody Bedlam, and you are just *bloody*."

"Suttons. Do not concern yourself. Jasper Sutton found out you were mucking about in the monkery with fancy coves, playing duke. He took the opportunity to strike. I have been fighting back."

There was much in his brother's snarled words which needed addressing.

"First, I was not mucking about in the countryside. Nor was I playing duke. Second, since when have I given you leave to start a war with the Suttons, Devil?" The last emerged from Dom as a bark.

"Seeing as how everything was falling apart in your absence and I had no notion of when you planned to return, it seemed the best course." Devil scowled at him. "What would you have me do? Allow The Devil's Spawn to fall into ruin?"

"And how is this not ruin?" Dom snapped. Ordinarily, he was close to his brother and loyal—mayhap even to a fault. However, this…it went beyond. "I have returned to gunfire and flames, smoke billowing out the windows, mayhem everywhere, my own brother bleeding from a wound above his eye…"

"This is not ruin. Ruin would be the whole place in ashes on the ground. Ruin would be you with your throat slit, Jasper Sutton dancing on your corpse."

"I am going to bloody well kill that worthless fucker for this," Dom spat.

"Leave it to Blade," Devil counseled. "The Suttons were behind another attack before this one, which is why I retaliated and burned down one of their warehouses. We will prove they were behind this one as well, and then we will go after them."

"This time, I am not going to stop until they are destroyed," Dom vowed. "Jasper Sutton will wish he had never been born when I am finished with him."

And to accomplish that, he was going to have to put his plan into motion sooner than he had previously envisioned.

He was going to have to see Adele's father, the Duke of Linross.

❄

"This is your home?"

Adele took in the sumptuous townhome with wide eyes.

"You've caught me, Duchess. I picked the lock and paid off the charleys. Hopefully the fine lord and lady who live here won't return for the next day or so."

Dom's sardonic drawl had her turning toward her husband. It did not escape her that she had returned to *Duchess* once more. Ever since the horrible, terrifying scene at his gaming hell earlier, he had been in a foul mood. She could well understand, for her own heart was still pounding.

Those endless moments in the carriage, awaiting his return, had seemed an eternity. She had been worried over his safety, terrified something would happen to him. Hands clasped in prayer. She had not realized until that moment, tired and worn from their journey, uncertain of whether or not her husband would return to her unscathed as he had promised, just how much she had already come to rely upon him.

Still, she had no intention of allowing him to resurrect the icy distance that had so recently existed between them. They were husband and wife. Over the last few weeks, more had changed than their marital status. They had grown closer, and her feelings for him…well, they had blossomed as well.

"You brought me to a gaming hell that was on fire and there were gunshots in the streets," she pointed out. "I hardly think the question unjustified."

His sensual lips tightened at the reminder. "It will not happen again. If I had known what was awaiting us, I would have brought you here directly."

"Why did you take me to The Devil's Spawn?" she inquired, curious. "Why not this place?"

He had told her he intended for her to live with him in the gaming hell, but why would he not choose instead to stay here, in elegance? The interior of the townhome—presumably his, though he had yet to outright confirm ownership—had taken her by complete surprise. It was outfitted sumptuously with fine furniture. Handsomely carved mahogany, enhanced by gilt, thick Aubusson beneath her slippers.

The rooms were spacious and hung with fresh wall coverings and gorgeous paintings. The chamber in which they stood was dominated by a cheval glass running from floor to ceiling. With a decorative gilt frame surrounding it featuring two winged goddesses at the top, each holding a rose outstretched as if in offering.

"I needed to make certain everything was running smoothly." Dom's wry voice interrupted her thoughts and wandering eye, jerking her attention back to him. "If I had supposed, for a moment, you and the babe would have been in danger, I would have brought you here first."

"I am glad you did not." She moved toward him, drawn to him as ever, as if there were some hidden force propelling them together. "If someone is trying to harm you, I want to know. I want to know everything there is about you, Dominic Winter. The good and the bad and the terrifying."

His lips twitched. "Ah, angel. What am I to do with you? You are too sweet for your own good, and far more than a wretch like me deserves."

No longer *Duchess*. For the first time in a long time, she was *angel* once more. Adele liked the sound of that. She dared to reach out and brush her hand slowly down his coat sleeve. It was torn and marred with soot and—unless she was mistaken—blood.

His or another's?

Adele gasped, forgetting her earlier question. In the tumult of his return to the carriage and their hasty retreat to the West End, she had somehow failed to take note of the stain. "Were you injured?"

He glanced down at the blood, looking unsurprised and unimpressed, as if blood on his sleeves were a commonplace occurrence. "Not mine. My brother's."

She inhaled again. "How badly was he hurt? That seems like a fair amount of blood."

"The beast will live. Genevieve had to stitch him up. I suppose I got some of his blood on me in the process. Someone has to hold him down. He has a violent reaction to the poke of a hot needle. Always has his whole life."

The calm manner in which he spoke of such matters—his brother being wounded deeply enough to require stitches, his sister being the one to administer the treatment, and Dom himself being forced to hold down his brother—had her confused once more. As confused as she was to be standing within the elegantly appointed chamber of this Mayfair townhome.

"This manner of unsettling circumstance happens…often…in your world?" she asked weakly, feeling rather ill at the notion of his poor sister having to thrust a needle through her brother's flesh.

"It *can* happen." His expression had gone grim. He shook off her touch and shrugged out of his jacket, tossing it to the floor. "If I have my way, it will never happen again."

Beneath the jacket, the lawn sleeve of his shirt was also stained an undeniable shade of crimson slowly fading to rust. He began undoing the buttons of his waistcoat next, flicking them from their moorings one by one. The marking on his hand caught her attention, that wicked dagger drawn between his thumb and forefinger.

"How can you make certain it will never happen again?"

"By seeing my enemies crushed as they deserve." He dropped his waistcoat to the floor, and then, he worked on the few buttons at the neck of his shirt. "Do not look so horrified, love. You knew what manner of man I was when you came to me the first time. You knew who I was when you married me, too. In my world, if I do not defeat my enemies, they will defeat me."

When he phrased it thus, she well understood his stance. And yet, it was all so horrific. So unlike the world into which she had been born. Still, for all that she was the daughter of a duke, the house in which they stood could have belonged to any lord.

She frowned at him, studying this handsome, perplexing enigma she had wed. "This is truly your home, then? I thought you meant for us to live above your gaming hell."

"I own this home and its contents." He finished the last button on his shirt and paused. "I do not like it. Never intended to live here. But today with Sutton, and you carrying our babe... Suffice it to say I'll suffer four walls befitting a nib to keep you safe."

He had revealed a mouthwatering expanse of his chest by sliding those buttons from their moorings. But still, not enough. She wanted to see him without his shirt from the front. In the light of day, with no shadows cloaking his body from her avid gaze.

How had she managed to get so distracted?

"Your shirtsleeve is stained as well," she told him softly. "You really ought to remove it for laundering."

In truth, she just wanted to see him, but she did not want to be so bold.

He grasped the tails of his shirt in both hands. "You are certain, Adele? My scars..."

"Take it off."

He inclined his head. "As my lady wishes."

In a fluid motion, he hauled the shirt over his head and tossed it to the floor, where it landed in a whisper of sound, atop his other discarded garments. Her mouth went dry. His scars were on vivid display, different from the lines on his back. These were jagged and far less precise, rained over his torso as if a vengeful god had placed them there. Beneath the signs of his life in the ruthless underworld of East London, his muscles were on stark display. His chest was broad, shaded with a fine smattering of masculine hair. On his biceps, he possessed another marking, this one a rose. On his chest, five letters were inked on his flesh in small, neat print. *DDBGG*. It took her but a moment to realize the letters must stand for the names of each of his siblings.

"Shocked, Duchess?"

His grim query cut through her rapt inspection of his naked upper body. "Pleased, Dom. Intrigued, as well. May I?"

He swallowed, his Adam's apple bobbing. "Aye."

She traced her fingers over the inking on his muscled arm first, tracing the flower. "How have you come to have these?"

"Also the work of Genevieve." He swallowed again, holding himself unnaturally still, his body tensed beneath her trailing fingertips. "She is skilled with needles. Nor does she swoon at the sight of blood as some of our brothers do."

"She draws this with ink and a needle?" Adele asked, fascinated. "Does it stay forever?"

"Forever, yes." His hand closed over hers. "It is a mark of honor."

"You love your siblings." It was a statement, not a question, for she could see how much he cared. She loved her sisters and brother fiercely as well, and she would do anything for them. His devotion to his family—or at least, the siblings he considered his true family—pleased her.

"They are my family."

Beneath her fingers, his heart beat a steady thump. How vital he was, the heat and strength of him seeping into her. The shock and fear that had assailed her earlier at his gaming hell returned.

"If something had happened to you today…" She trailed off, unable to complete her sentence. Though they had been wed for mere days and he had only been a part of her life for a handful of months, he had quickly become…essential.

There was no other way to describe him, no more suiting word.

"If something happens to me, you will be looked after, Adele," he said, plucking her hand from his chest and lifting it to his lips for a kiss. "My family is yours now. You are one of us, and I will fight like hell to make certain my enemies cannot hurt me, you, or any one of us. I do not want you to fear. That is why I brought you here, to a place I have scarcely spent any time, to a house I never expected to occupy. I want you safe, and I want to be here for you and our babe. I had no father and my mother was…scarcely better than my absent sire. I will not allow our child to suffer the same. Do you believe me?"

His sudden question took her aback, for she felt as if there remained so much she did not understand. So much she needed to learn and know. About her husband, his world, the dangers swirling around him.

But for now, she would answer him. "I believe you, Dom."

"And do you trust me?"

She did not hesitate. "Yes. I do."

As she said the words, she recognized the veracity of them. Dominic Winter may be a criminal, but there was good in his heart. He was a man who cared, a man who felt strongly.

"Good." He dropped a kiss upon her lips, hasty and quick. Far too quickly for her liking. "I am going to teach you how to wield a blade and shoot a pistol."

❆

"Hold the dagger with a firm grip, and make certain you keep your fingers behind the guard. Your intent is to harm your opponent and not yourself."

Dom's voice was soft and low, his fingers curled over hers on the hilt of the weapon. He was positioned at her back, the strength and heat of him seeming to burn her through the layers of her gown and petticoat. Adele was not sure which she found more disconcerting—her husband's nearness, the fact that he was teaching her how to wound an enemy, or that said lessons were being conducted in a drawing room laden with gilt and sleek mahogany and rosewood.

The drawing room was as fine as any she had ever seen. Blue French curtains adorned the windows, with a panel of fashionable fringe and tassels suspended from gilt rosettes. The chairs were fashioned of carved mahogany and covered in rich damask silk that matched the window dressings to perfection. A colossal circular ottoman made of matching wood and damask dominated the far wall. It was piled with cushions and ornamented with bronze and carved swans. Everything about the chamber suggested it had recently been abandoned by a fine lord or lady, and yet it was all…new.

"When you acquired this house, was it furnished?" she asked.

"Damn it, Duchess, have you listened to a bloody word I've said?" he growled in her ear.

Strangely, even his displeasure sent sparks shooting through her. "I am listening, but I will admit to being a trifle distracted. You cannot deny the events of today have proven most unexpected."

And that was a profound understatement. The chaos awaiting them at The Devil's Spawn had yet to be fully explained to her. Their arrival at a home in Mayfair had been shocking enough, but lessons in pistols and knives?

He released his grip on her hand, leaving her holding the blade on her own, and spun Adele about to face him. The sudden movement had her dizzied. She nearly dropped the blade.

"Listen to me." His expression was harsh and unreadable. "My enemies are also yours, and they have just shown they are willing to go to great lengths to destroy me. I cannot be at your side at all times, and I need to know you will be prepared if they should somehow find their way through the guards I have in place here and find you."

His warning sent a shiver through her. "You truly believe I will be unsafe here?"

Had he issued the warning in the East End, she would have believed him. But Mayfair? It was impossible to believe the darkness and dangers of his world could exist here.

"I hope not. However, we must prepare. My enemy slashed my brother's face and nearly burned The Devil's Spawn to the ground. He is capable of anything."

The reminder filled her with a renewed grip of nausea, but this time it had nothing to do with her condition and everything to do with fear.

She nodded. "I will learn."

"There's my angel." He nodded approvingly. "Hold the dagger in a firm grip and raise it toward me."

She did as he asked, hating that she was pointing it in his direction.

"Now imagine you are drawing an imaginary X with the

tip of your blade."

Slowly, Adele moved the blade, fashioning an *X*.

"Draw a cross."

She changed the direction of the dagger, drawing a cross pattern over and over.

"You need to move with strength and determination. Pretend I am your enemy, coming for you, intending to do you harm. Your blade work would not harm a goddamn butterfly."

His cutting observation shook her. Not for the first time, it occurred to her how ill-prepared she was for this marriage, this man. She was the daughter of a duke. She had been raised for ballrooms and embroidery and carriage rides in the park. She had never held a blade in her hand before today, nor had she ever imagined the need to wield one.

"I am disappointing you," she said quietly. "I am sorry."

"Do not apologize, damn you. Try harder." He scowled. "You need to slash him. Begin at the top. Wound him at the most vulnerable place, his throat. Do as much damage as you can manage."

"I am not certain I can do it, Dom." The notion of striking another with the intent to kill or harm, even in her own defense, made her ill.

"You can do anything. You are the woman who burst into The Devil's Spawn and demanded an audience with me. That woman is fearless."

His impassioned words gave her the spur she needed. He was right. She had been brave then. She had never intended to become a part of his world, but she was now. There was no denying it.

Adele nodded and went through the motions he had showed her, the *X* and the cross. This time, she put more force into her motions.

Dom nodded. "Good, now thrust the blade, then slash. Thrust toward the throat, slash down his coat. Do not show him mercy."

Biting her lip, she copied his movements, thrusting the blade toward an invisible enemy, then slashing downward. Again and again, she repeated the action. Suddenly, he struck. He caught her wrist in a punishing grip, and her fingers opened. The dagger fell to the carpets with a thud. Dom hauled her to him, his face near hers, his eyes blazing with an emotion she could not define.

"If I were Jasper Sutton, you would be dead by now," he said.

There was a finality in his voice that made her tremble. "Is that his name? Your enemy, I mean?"

His lip curled. "It does not matter what his name is. All that matters is that you need more practice. If anything should happen to you or the babe…"

As his words trailed off, Adele absorbed the answering tremor that went through him. There was no denying it. He cared. Dominic Winter, feared ruler of London's underworld, *cared* for her. The knowledge settled firmly in her heart.

"Nothing shall happen to us," she promised him. "Show me, Dom."

He gave a jerky nod, then dipped his head and took her lips in a kiss that was hard and possessive, yet fierce and sweet.

Much like the man she had married.

Chapter Thirteen

❈

"SHE WILL HATE you for this."

Dom skewered Devil with a glare as they stood together in his office at The Devil's Spawn, a map spread on the desk before them. "Why should I give a damn? This course has been planned, its outcome inevitable."

"You truly think Linross will be any more inclined to sell the land knowing you've married his precious daughter?"

His brother's skepticism nettled. At the moment, Dom felt like sparring with someone. Boxing until his knuckles bled. Or hunting down Jasper Sutton and sinking his knife deep into the bastard's guts. Watching his life blood seep into the dirt.

He told himself the fury lancing him had nothing to do with Devil's assertion Adele would hate him when she learned his true motive for marrying her. And then he realized what an utter fucking lie that was.

"If Linross does not sell me the land, I will call in all his son's notes," Dom vowed, even as a foreign twinge of something in his chest accompanied those words.

Not guilt, surely?

When had he ever allowed himself to feel anything for anyone other than his siblings?

Since she came into your life.

"You would call in the brother's notes and ruin 'im?"

Devil asked. "A nib, your wife's brother?"

Wife was still a new word, bringing with it more strange sensations in his chest. Ruthlessly, he tamped them down, clinging instead to his rage.

"I will do what I have to do," he told Dom. "Jasper Sutton's grip on the water supply and the East End has to be ended. If we do not crush him, he will crush us. His recent actions show that, and I have far too much to lose now."

"Her?" Devil sneered.

His disgust for the quality was abundant and bitter. Dom's had been the same, until a dark-haired, dark-eyed duke's daughter had entered his life. Before Adele, Dom had considered aristocrats pawns. Plump, entitled pigeons. He had never given a damn about the losses they suffered at his tables. The borders were clear between their worlds, and Dom did not cross. It was one of the reasons he had chosen not to live in the Mayfair house.

"You do not know her as I do," he said to Devil, struggling to explain. "She is not like the others."

Devil grunted. "Course she is."

"Damn you, Devil." He slammed his fist on the map, crinkling it in the place where he intended to build the B.W. Waterworks. Just as soon as the Duke of Linross sold him the eleven bloody acres he required surrounding the River Lea. "Lady Adele is different."

Devil's sole response was to growl.

"She is carrying my child," Dom blurted.

His brother issued another grunt.

"Is that felicitations I hear in your voice, brother?"

"Sympathy." Devil made another sound that was half-growl, half-grunt. "Speaking of waifs, that little shite you dragged home from the monkery stole my pocket watch."

Well, damn. He had been hoping the lad would practice

his talents on those outside the hell. Dom would have to have a talk with him. Still, if he was daring enough to trouble Devil, it was a good sign.

He flashed his brother a grin. "His name is Davy."

"Ought to be Satan," Devil muttered.

Dom chuckled, but his amusement faded as his attention returned to the map. "Buying the land and offering competition to Sutton is the only way we can ease his grip on the people."

Devil made another low sound in his throat. "We can kill him."

Dom nodded. "When the time is right, we will strike." He sent Devil another sidelong glance. "You truly think she will hate me?"

"Do rats live in the East End?"

Never one to coat his words in honey, Devil Winter.

It would seem no matter what he did, Dom was bloody well doomed.

❉

"YOU ARE CERTAIN we must do this now?" Adele asked her husband as they waited in the entry hall of her father's townhome while the butler announced their arrival to her father.

Breaking the news of their nuptials was necessary, she knew. But with all the tumult of the last few days and them only having arrived back in London the day before, seeing her father with such haste made her stomach tighten into a knot.

"Your father must be informed of our marriage," Dom said at her side, his voice a low, soothing rumble.

Yes, but why today?

Why ever?

Father would be livid. He may never speak to her again. Her siblings would be shocked. Mama would be properly horrified. Misery swamped her.

"He must, yes," she agreed, taking in the familiar confines of the entry hall as if she were a guest. Noticing new details which must have always been present and yet which she had never taken the time to note.

"Are you ashamed of me, Duchess?"

Adele's gaze flew to her handsome husband. To look at him—dressed elegantly in a dark coat and waistcoat with buff breeches and a perfectly knotted cravat—one would never know he had been born to the rough world of the East End. Still, there remained a wicked, commanding air about him. She was certain his walking stick carried a secreted blade. There was a brace of pistols hidden in their carriage.

And yet, she was not ashamed of him. Rather, she was proud of him. Proud of the kindness he was capable of showing. Of the hidden parts of himself he had revealed to her.

"I am not ashamed of you, Dom," she said softly. "I swear it to you."

His nostrils flared, and he nodded once, as if he had been awaiting her response. As if he had been uncertain of what she would say. Her heart gave a pang. He was not as self-assured and untouchable as she had once believed.

Before they could indulge in further conversation, the butler returned, directing them to her father's study. They were scarcely over the threshold when her father stalked toward them, his face red.

He was furious.

"What is the meaning of this, my lady? Bringing this brute as accompaniment? Your reputation will be in ruins if word of this should go beyond these walls."

She had never stood up to her father. Adele was the quiet twin. The one everyone underestimated. But she was more than the wallflower she had been painted.

Dom tensed at her side, and Adele knew he wanted to speak on her behalf. Her hand on his coat sleeve was all that was required to shake him from his course. She sent him a telling look, hoping he could understand what she wished to convey to him.

Let me handle my father.

He searched her gaze, his jaw hardening, but in the end, her fierce and dangerous husband nodded and held his tongue.

Gratitude swept over her, along with the rush of another sensation, stronger and more potent than what she had felt before. Warm and unexpected.

Love.

She fell in love with Dominic Winter as they stood before her disapproving father. The realization stole her breath for a heartbeat, but it also gave her strength. Courage. Determination to go on.

A voice with which to speak.

She turned her attention back to her formidable sire. "Mr. Winter is my husband, Father."

"The devil he is." Her father surged toward Dom, as if he intended to physically attack him.

Dom sidestepped her father's advances neatly, a mocking grin on his lips she recognized too well. Here was the mask he donned for strangers. He was the fearsome Dominic Winter, hard and harsh and merciless.

"I would take care if I were you, Linross," he said. "Doing me harm is a right dangerous proposition. If my men were to discover, you could not run fast enough or hide yourself well enough from their retribution."

Father stopped. "Do you dare to threaten me, you despicable mongrel?"

Adele had never heard such vitriol from her father before. It was almost as if he were familiar with Dom. But...how could that be?

"I married Mr. Winter, Father," she repeated. "It is true. I apologize for the haste with which our nuptials occurred, but it was unavoidable, I fear. I was unintentionally compromised at the house party, and we were left with no choice."

"Compromised? You?" Her father sneered. "A quiet girl such as you has nothing to recommend her save your face, and believe me, a pretty face is not what a bastard like him is seeking."

She frowned at her father's cruel, caustic words. "If you think Mr. Winter seeks my dowry, you are wrong. He has more than enough of his own funds."

Still, whilst she did not believe him to have married her for financial benefit, she remained uncertain of why he had. A man such as he had no need to wed. As he had told her himself, he was not the sort of man who sought societal acceptance or *entrée* to balls. Rather, he was a law unto his own.

And yet, he had not answered her whenever she had asked him why he had wanted to marry her.

"It is not your dowry he is after, you foolish chit," her father snapped, his voice echoing in the eerie calm of the chamber with the force of a slap. "You did not truly think he would want to marry you, did you? Evie is a diamond of the first water, with a legion of gentlemen begging to court her. You have no suitors to speak of."

She flinched. That was not entirely true. She'd had suitors...not many, it was true. She had grown accustomed to living in her beautiful twin's shadow, to allowing Evie to speak for her.

"Take care how you speak to my wife, Linross," Dom growled. "I protect what is mine."

"She is not yours, you spurious cur!" Father's face went a mottled shade of red. "You have done this to spite me. To force my hand, have you not? I will have this marriage annulled, and you can have what you want. I will sell you the land for your waterworks."

Everything inside Adele seemed to freeze. And then, like autumn flowers who had suffered the first fatal kiss of frost, shriveled.

She turned to her husband, feeling numb. "You and my father are acquainted?"

Dom inclined his head. "We are. I have been attempting to buy a parcel of land from Linross for the last year. He has thwarted me at every turn."

"And now, when he could not get what he wanted, he has involved you in his plans." Her father sneered at Dom. "Leave my daughter out of this, you pathetic weasel. I will sell you the land, and then I hope to never see you again."

Her mind could scarcely seem to comprehend the scene unfolding before her. Dom had never told her he knew her father, nor that he had been attempting to purchase land from him. What could all this mean?

She searched her husband's grim countenance. "Is what my father says true? You wish to buy land from him?"

"It is true that I want to buy the land for a waterworks in the East End. It is also true that he refused to sell me the parcel out of spite. He does not deem me suitable enough to acquire the land, even by legal means."

His acknowledgment only made the cold inside her blossom, overtaking her. "So you decided to marry me so you could force my father's hand and have your waterworks?"

He reached for her, the harsh lines in his expression softening. "Adele, all is not as it seems. Trust me."

Trust him?

She stared at his big, outstretched hand, wondering if she dared.

His jaw hardened. "Adele, please. Give me a chance to explain."

"Whatever has happened, we will see the marriage annulled. If he has forced you or importuned you in any fashion, I will bring the law down upon him," her father interrupted.

"Trust me, Adele," Dom entreated, repeating those three words.

"You cannot trust him," Father snapped. "He is a liar and a thief and a murderer. You have no notion of the trouble you have just caused for yourself. For us all. I knew allowing you to attend that house party without your mother's careful guidance was a mistake. And then, for your sister to abandon you there with those wretched people. Those cursed Winters."

He said the surname as if it were an epithet.

"You cannot annul the marriage," Dom said then, his tone firm and angry. "Lady Adele is carrying my child."

Her father paled. "You cannot be certain of such a state already. I will have her examined by my physician."

"You will do no such thing," roared Dom, his tone lethal as he stalked toward her father. "She is my wife."

"Dom, please." Adele went after him, seizing his arm, staying him when he would have approached her father.

She had no wish for her father and her husband to come to fisticuffs or worse. Dom Winter was a strong, virile man. Her father could not possibly defend himself.

He looked at her, fury evident in every line of his handsome countenance. "I will not allow him to have you defiled by some physician. You are my wife. There will be no annulment. You have a choice to make, Adele. Will it be me, or will it be your father?"

Adele searched his stare, hearing anew the anguish in his voice when he had spoken yesterday. *If anything should happen to you or the babe...*

He cared for her, for their child. She knew he did. And whatever his reason for keeping this a secret from her, there was no denying the way she felt for him.

Dom's gaze remained fierce upon her, searing. He awaited her answer.

"She will choose what is right and proper, of course," her father intervened. "Lady Adele is the daughter of a duke. Although this regrettable marriage of yours will mean she is soiled goods, I can find someone to wed her. A baron or a country squire. Anyone would be better than a mongrel like you. Come now, Adele. Step away from Winter."

"No," she managed.

Because she could not choose anyone else over him. He was her husband, the father of her child.

The man she loved.

"No?" her father spat, as if he could not believe his ears.

"No," she repeated firmly. The wallflower had found her voice. She was making her decision. She entwined her arm through Dominic's. "I am married to Mr. Winter, and you must accept it."

Her husband's hand closed over hers. "I will see that everything is sent to you concerning the property."

"There will be no sale of the property without an annulment." Her father's voice was frigid.

"If there is no sale without an annulment, I will be forced to call in all Lord Sundenbury's debts."

Adele stiffened at the mention of her brother.

Her father did as well. "You lowborn bastard. I will see

you ruined if you try anything so despicable."

Her husband inclined his head. "I think you will be selling me the land, Linross. You have two days."

He sketched an ironic bow, and Adele forced herself to curtsy. She was still feeling numb as he propelled her from the room, leaving her father stewing behind them.

❄

THEY WERE SCARCELY settled in the carriage when his wife spoke.

"You told me that if I married you, you would forgive my brother his debts," she accused.

Her expression was pinched, but he did not think he espied hatred there as Devil had been so certain he would. Instead, it was something worse. She appeared...wounded.

He hated her pain. Hated being the cause of it. This was what happened each day, was it not? Darkness surpassed the light, and the sun was extinguished. Still, it did not feel right. Hurting Adele felt as if he had swallowed a rock, and it was lodged uncomfortably in his stomach.

"I have returned some of your brother's debts," he allowed. "But not all."

"Then you lied to me."

Her voice was like a lash. Shame accompanied it, stinging, burning.

"I did not lie about the debts," he countered, for it was truth. "All his debts, up until the time we wed, have been returned to him. Unfortunately, Sundenbury has not ceased tempting fortune. His debts continue to mount."

"And you have been buying them all."

Once again, his wife was observant. Intelligent.

He nodded. "Indirectly, yes."

"To strongarm my father into selling you the land you require," she finished for him.

"My initial plan was to use you both," he admitted, hating himself for the way it sounded.

Then wondering why. Dominic Winter showed no mercy. He possessed no compunction. He did what he had to do, and he never made apologies for it. It was what had kept him alive and made him one of the most powerful men in the East End.

"That is why you married me," she guessed. "You intended to trade me for the land."

He wished for a trap door to spring open in the floor of his carriage so he could fall into it. "Yes. Eventually."

Her hand crept to her abdomen in a protective gesture. "You changed your mind when you discovered I am carrying your child, however."

"No." He shook his head. "I changed my mind as soon as I saw you again in Oxfordshire. I had been looking for you everywhere, searching all London. I told myself the entire journey that I would hold true to my plan. That it was a boon the gorgeous angel I had not been capable of forgetting all these months was also the daughter to the man who would not sell me the land I needed."

"You ought to have told me then, when you arrived in Oxfordshire."

"A gentleman would have," he acknowledged. "But as we have already established, I am no gentleman. And if I had told you the truth, you never would have married me."

"I do not know what I would have done, but you stole the choice from me, Dom," she said, her tone enough to slay him.

"I am sorry."

How those three words emerged from his own lips was a mystery. Dom did not make apologies.

Adele's lips parted, revealing her surprise as well. "You are sorry."

"I am sorry for...manipulating you," he elaborated with painstaking precision. "I was wrong. I am a man who is accustomed to taking what he wants and not giving a damn about the consequences. But that does not make what I did right."

She nodded, her lips compressing to a fine, grim line once more. "Go on."

She wanted to know everything, his curious wife. Of course she did. Fair enough.

He passed a hand over his jaw, finding the place to begin. "Jasper Sutton owns Sutton Waterworks, which provides water to a large portion of the area surrounding The Devil's Spawn. The bastard has a monopoly, but his rates are high and the quality of water he provides is poor. I am aiming to create a rival waterworks that will have cleaner water and fairer prices. The water at The Devil's Spawn will no longer come from a suspect source. However, the land I need, where I must build reservoirs surrounding the River Lea, is owned by the Duke of Linross, a man who has refused to sell for the last year."

Her brows drew together. "Were you truly responsible for my brother's beating? Was that a lie as well?"

"That was Sutton, just as I told you. Your brother was in deep at Sutton's tables, and Suttons are notoriously merciless. They would as soon cut a nib as one of their own. After you came to me and disappeared, I began buying up your brother's vowels. At first, it was to find you. Then, when I discovered who you truly were, my plan became twofold."

"Will you truly ruin my brother if my father will not sell you the land?" she wanted to know next.

He sighed. The Dominic Winter he had been before

would have done so, without a modicum of guilt. The man he had become, however, was not so certain.

"I want the land," he said instead of answering her query. "I need that land."

"How will having the land solve your quarrels with Sutton? Will it keep him from attempting to burn down your gaming hell again?"

"No," he admitted. If anything, starting a rival waterworks would only heighten the enmity between himself and Jasper Sutton.

So, too, the danger.

"Please do not do this, Dom."

Her soft plea did strange things to him.

"Duchess," he began.

"I love you," she blurted.

And the heart Dom had sworn he no longer possessed swelled inside his chest, until it felt too big for his stupid body.

Floating hell.

He had misheard her. He would have suspected the aftereffects of poison, rendering him delusional, but Devereaux Winter was nowhere in sight.

"I love you," she repeated, leaving no doubts as to what she had just said. "I want a true marriage with you, and I want my family to accept you. Given time, I believe they will. But there cannot be hatred and distance between us. This cannot be the way we begin things."

She was asking him to give up his plans for the waterworks.

Impossible.

Or was it?

The beautiful, elegant lady staring at him expectantly from across the conveyance loved him. More honey and lightness filled him, chasing his darkness. Replacing it.

And he found himself offering a concession for the first time in his bloody life. "For you, I will try to find another way, angel."

Chapter Fourteen

"YOU ARE A fucking Bedlamite."

The proclamation, issued by his brother Demon, was nothing Dom himself had not been thinking.

Devil grunted.

"We ought to slice his throat in his sleep," Blade offered.

Dom was afraid to ask if Blade was referring to himself or to the man they were about to welcome deep into their territory for the first time. Blade was the assassin amongst them, and he was also the least enthusiastic of all Dom's siblings concerning his new plan.

"If he dares to make a wrong move, I will beat him to a bloody pulp," Gavin added, lifting his tremendous fists—merciless weapons in his boxing matches—in warning.

"What I cannot believe is that the lot of you intended to welcome a blackleg like Jasper Sutton to The Devil's Spawn without me," Genevieve said. "Especially since you invited *him*."

The *him* Dom's golden-haired sister referred to was none other than Devereaux Winter. Brother dearest. Spoiled, arrogant sod. And just the help they needed for what they were about to do.

Dom would not lie. Having to approach Winter with his tail betwixt his legs had bloody well stung worse than smuggled Scots whisky poured over an open wound.

"My presence is required," Winter said mildly. "Like it or not, I am a half brother to you all."

Devil growled.

Demon sniffed.

Gavin glared.

Blade withdrew a knife and ran his thumb down the beveled edge.

Genevieve gave an indelicate snort. "Fine half brother you are, only appearing when there is coin to be gained."

She was dressed in her standard garb of breeches, polished boots, shirt and waistcoat, complete with a cravat. Genevieve was a dab hand at tying knots, in addition to working a needle. Though she'd deny it with her last breath.

"Calm yourself, Gen," Dom cautioned his hot-tempered sister. "We spoke about this. Mr. Winter is aiding us when he does not need to be. He owns a property at the docks Sutton is keen to get his hands on, and he is willing to sell that to help our cause."

"Meaning that spider-arsed scoundrel always gets what he wants," Genevieve said, scowling.

Devereaux Winter drummed his fingers on the desk they had all gathered around. "Might I suggest you avoid calling our friend *spider-arsed* in his presence? What does such an insult mean, if you do not mind my asking?"

Genevieve raised a superior brow. "Have one look at Jasper Sutton, and you'll know exactly what."

Genevieve's inability to control her tongue had been one of the reasons Dom and his brothers had not initially informed her about this meeting. Another had been her intense dislike for Devereaux Winter, a man whom Dom had to admit was not nearly as horrible of a nib as he'd thought. Brother dearest was actually beginning to grow on him. Much like Davy.

"I hope you can keep your minion under control today," Demon added, as if reading Dom's thoughts. "The little shite stole my favorite pair of boots and then tipped me the Dublin packet before I could catch him."

Ah, young Davy. Dom was going to have to have *another* talk with the lad.

Devereaux Winter frowned. "What is this packet you are speaking of?"

"Here now. *Tipped the Dublin packet* is what we say when a thief gets away," explained Blade, still stroking his knife.

"If he tries to filch from Jasper Sutton, he will learn his lesson, won't he?" Genevieve chimed in.

Dom was beginning to get restless. A quick consult of his pocket watch revealed the time had drawn near to the arrival of Jasper Sutton. Ten of their best men were on the door today, awaiting the enemy's arrival. Part of Dom was still amazed Sutton had accepted his request for a meeting.

He suspected Sutton's decision had a great deal more to do with the promised presence of the indisputably wealthy and powerful Devereaux Winter than it had to do with aught else.

Dom tipped his head toward brother dearest. "I owe you my thanks for your willingness to offer us aid."

Winter nodded. "My lovely wife has persuaded me I must be less unyielding. She believes our family will be stronger united than torn asunder, and I rather think she is right."

An olive branch. The Dominic Winter of before would have broken it in half and tossed it in his half brother's face. The man he was now quietly accepted it. Because Adele would want him to, but also because it was the right thing to do.

Floating, fucking hell.

Fancy that.

"We are all Winters," Dom agreed.

The resulting silence from his siblings was only interrupted by the announcement that Jasper Sutton had arrived. Mayhap the rest of them would require more time. Mayhap this change was something only love could bring about.

Because, aye, there was one reason and one reason alone Dom was about to meet with Jasper Sutton. He was in love with his wife. Desperately, irrefutably, ridiculously in love.

Demon was not wrong in his assertion. He *was* a Bedlamite.

Jasper Sutton stood on the threshold then. Every Winter in the chamber drew to his and her respective feet.

"Search him," Dom told Devil.

His brother grunted and moved to Sutton.

"No weapons on me," Sutton said.

"All the same, I will believe my brother's word over yours," Dom said brightly, watching as Devil performed a thorough search, seeking any hidden weapons.

At Devil's nod, introductions resumed. Everyone sat down, but the air in the room was decidedly on edge although Sutton was unarmed. Tall, dark-haired, and menacing, Jasper Sutton ruled over his portion of the East End with an unforgiving fist.

"Well if it isn't Devereaux Winter 'imself." Sutton grinned, pleased. "Finally, a meeting."

Winter's dislike was ill-concealed. "Let us make this meeting quick, shall we? I know what you want, and you know what I want."

"Right." Sutton's eyes narrowed. "But what's the other Winters got to do with any of it?"

"You want to buy a warehouse Mr. Winter owns by the docks," Dom said. "But Mr. Winter is family."

Sutton's look was one of ill-disguised disbelief. Like any common surname, the sharing of it did not necessarily signify a familial relationship, and he had done his damnedest to keep his family separate from the legitimate Winters ever since discovering the connection.

"The fancy cove Winters and the East End Winters." Sutton guffawed.

"Yes," Devereaux Winter confirmed.

"We shared a sire," added Blade, who had begun spinning the point of his dagger upon the polished surface of Dom's desk.

Dom would box his ears for that later.

"All of you?"

"Every, last one, you spider—"

"All twelve of us," Dom interrupted, shooting his sister a warning glare.

One wrong word, and this entire deal could be over before it had begun. He had promised Adele he would find another way to solve his problem, and this was the way, *damn it*.

"I will give you the warehouse in question in exchange for the Sutton Waterworks and the promise you will cease all further attempts upon the Winter family and our properties," said Devereaux Winter, likely seeing the need to propel this meeting forward before it grew any more untenable.

"That's too high a bloody price," growled Sutton. "And I ain't taking the blame for the fires set here. That wasn't me. I will sell you the Waterworks. Only you, Winter. Not the rest of these twats. For two thousand pounds and the warehouse."

"Five hundred pounds and the warehouse, along with your promise," Devereaux Winter countered.

Dom had known, all along, that Sutton would not sell the Waterworks to anyone other than Deveraux Winter. He had known, too, his rival's keen interest in Winter's dock warehouse. In turn, Devereaux had agreed to divert the funds which had been held in trust since their father's death to the purchase of the waterworks and the sale of the warehouse. It would all be legally binding, but Sutton would not be pleased when he realized he had been outfoxed.

A problem Dom would deal with later, if the time came.

"One thousand, the warehouse, and I promise to stay away from The Devil's Spawn," Sutton said. "All of you."

"Done." Devereaux nodded. "I will have the papers drawn up."

Bloody hell.

It was done.

The waterworks would be theirs, and Dom could make peace with Adele's family as she wished.

"This better be worth it," grumbled Genevieve sourly.

It would be. Dom had no doubt.

❄

ADELE WAS HAVING the most divine dream.

The sun was bathing her in a golden light, and her husband's hand was moving up and down her spine in a warm, steady caress. His lips were on her ear.

"I love you, angel."

"Mmm," she purred, feeling like a cat being stroked.

"I have something I need to tell you."

That sounded far too serious for a lovely dream. But then he started kissing her neck just where she loved him to press his lips most. She sighed and arched her back, trying to get herself nearer to that delicious warmth.

"Wake up, love."

He nuzzled her throat.

A hand cupped her breast, expert fingers finding her hard nipple and tugging.

She wanted his mouth on her there. His tongue.

She rolled to her back and into a wall of solid masculinity. Bright light pierced her lashes, rocking her from the vestiges of slumber altogether. She blinked sleepily to find Dom stretched out beside her in bed, fully clothed, a tender smile on his sensual lips.

She cupped his cheek, a potent surge of emotion hitting her. "I love you."

Since she had revealed her feelings to him a fortnight ago in the carriage on their way home from her father's house, she had repeated the words to him often. Each time, he seemed surprised. Humbled. She could not say them enough, and he deserved to hear them. In time, she could only hope he would return them to her.

She had a patient heart.

She could wait.

"I love you, Adele."

She blinked. "Am I still dreaming?"

"Not dreaming, I hope." He grinned, his dark gaze burning into hers with such undisguised reverence and tenderness she could scarcely breathe. "I love you."

"Dom." She could not manage another word past the emotions clogging her throat. She clasped his face with both her hands in lieu of speaking and hauled his mouth to hers.

The kiss was long, slow, sweet. Filled with promise. Awareness settled between her thighs, made her breasts tingle and her nipples tighten. By the time their mouths parted, she was convinced she was awake.

And that her husband had just told her he *loved* her.

She had not been dreaming.

"I have news," he said, caressing her hair.

She could not resist the urge to rub her cheek against his palm. "Go on. Tell me."

"Jasper Sutton is selling the waterworks to Devereaux Winter. Winter has also extracted a promise from him that he will not further attack any Winters or Winter holdings."

Hope crept into her heart. "What does this mean?"

"It means, my darling wife, that I do not need your father's land. Nor do I need to use your brother's vowels. Devereaux Winter is purchasing the Sutton Waterworks using the trust our father set aside for the bastard Winters. We will control it, and we will be able to provide our people with better quality water at a lower price. Jasper Sutton gets the warehouse he wanted, and we have our safety and freedom."

She searched his gaze, noting, not for the first time, the flecks of gold and cinnamon hidden within their rich depths. "Does this mean we will return to The Devil's Spawn to live?"

"Not unless you wish it." He kissed her again, swiftly. "With you here, this house feels like home for the first time."

She smiled, tears threatening her vision. "I feel the same way."

Not that she would not have lived above his gaming hell if he wished it, but with the attempts that had been made on the building and a babe on the way…this home seemed safer. It seemed more *theirs*. A place where they could start anew, grow both their family and their love.

"And now, I ought to leave you to your nap, since you are in a delicate condition," he said, dropping a kiss upon her lips, then another on her nose and yet another on her forehead. "You need your rest."

Rest had been wonderful whilst he had been gone, but rest was the last thing on Adele's mind now. When he would have left the bed, she clutched his arms, holding him there. "Do not go. I do not think rest is what my delicate condition needs just now."

A slow, wicked smile curved his lips. "Oh? And what is it

your delicate condition *does* need, Mrs. Winter?"

She grinned back at him. "Nothing but *you*, Mr. Winter." Adele tugged her husband's mouth back to hers.

Epilogue

❄

*T*HE EXCITED SHRIEKS emerging from the drawing room lured Adele like a Siren's song. She had been indulging in an afternoon nap, but as was oft the case, her quiet had been interrupted by the happy din of Dom and their children. She paused on the threshold, cradling her belly, watching the melee unfolding within.

Georgianna and Colin were wielding wooden swords. Tessa was seated upon a cushion on the floor, small carved horses laid before her as if they pulled her in a carriage.

"We shall protect you from the beast!" shouted Colin, raising his sword and narrowly missing knocking a vase from a nearby rosewood table.

Dom suddenly popped up from behind the circular ottoman. "Did I hear someone say beast?"

He punctuated his question with a mighty roar that had their children squealing wildly.

Adele could not suppress her smile or the uncontrollable flood of love rushing through her. There was her heart, on display. She took a moment to drink in the sight of them—the three little dark-haired children, their grins so like her husband's, the unabashed love and delight on Dom's handsome countenance. He had a counterpane wrapped around his broad shoulders as if it were a cloak.

As she watched, he spread his arms wide and roared again,

moving for the children who made more elated sounds of mock horror. In one swoop, he covered them all with the blanket, fashioning a tent around them.

"Now I have you all where I want you," he announced, his voice muffled by the fabric. "Princess, I shall begin by tickling you! And fearless guards, I will divest you of your swords and tickle you as well."

"Never!" shouted Colin.

"We shall not be tickled!" declared Georgianna.

Tessa erupted into a fit of giggles that suggested her papa was indeed tickling her.

Adele blinked away the tears of happiness clouding her vision. Ever since she had found herself in a delicate condition with their fourth child, she could not seem to stop turning into a watering pot over the smallest moments. But she could not help it. Her heart was so full, her life spilling over with happiness.

The fearsome Dominic Winter was a wonderful father. She had always known he would be, of course. Some may have doubted. Her own family certainly had. But Dom had proven himself again and again. He was honorable, steadfast, and loving, loyal and protective. She never could have known on the day she had first sought him out that she would end up finding the other half of herself, the part that had been missing.

More giggling rang beneath the counterpane, Dom's laugh mingling with their children's, until at last he threw back the blanket. Their children were rosy-cheeked and grinning. Her husband's warm gaze met hers.

"Mama! You are finished with your nap already?" he asked, grinning.

"How is one to sleep with all this noise?" she asked, smiling back at him. "I heard there was a beast in the drawing room that was tickling the princess and her fearless guards, and I had to investigate for myself."

"Papa is so silly!" Tessa announced, before dissolving into laughter once more.

"He is a tickle beast," Colin added sagely.

"But he is no match for our swords," Georgianna added, brandishing her sword. "Look, Mama. Papa has been giving me lessons."

Her daughter drew an *X* in the air.

Adele was reminded of a time, long ago, when he had given her similar lessons. There was no fear of reprisals from enemies now, however. Their lives had settled into a comfortable routine, and she was glad for it. The rivalry between the Winters and the Suttons had been settled.

"Quite formidable, Georgianna," she praised her daughter.

"He has been teaching me also." Colin proceeded to show off his sword skills as well.

This time, he gave the vase a sound thwack, and it hurtled to the floor.

"Oh dear! Sorry, Mama." Her son's small face crumpled, tears instantly swimming in his eyes.

He had such a sensitive heart, much like his papa.

Dom retrieved the vase and settled it back on the table. "No harm done. Nary even a crack in it, lad."

"Come here," Adele said, opening her arms wide. "All of you."

Her family raced toward her. Three little sets of arms wrapped around Adele instantly, and another set of arms, large and strong, gently encircled her.

"I love you," she told them, unable to keep the tears from rolling down her cheeks now. Her heart was bursting.

"We love you too, angel."

Warm, knowing lips found hers.

❄

Dom kissed his beloved wife, his heart beating with more happiness than any man had a right to feel. Her belly was full and round between them, carrying their fourth child who would arrive soon. Georgianna, Colin, and Tessa surrounded them, embracing both him and their mama's skirts.

Her lips were silken and soft, moving beneath his, telling him without words everything she felt. He cupped her face, breaking the kiss to stare down at her loveliness.

Gratitude hit him, and with it came that warm trickle in his chest, much like honey. Filling and overflowing.

"Am I dreaming?" he asked her softly, an old joke between them now.

Sometimes, it certainly felt as if he were.

"Not dreaming," she said, echoing the words he had told her years ago, her smile beautiful.

Floating hell, that smile hit him directly in the heart, like an arrow.

"Good," he whispered.

And then he kissed his wife again as they stood in the drawing room he had never imagined would one day ring with such love and laughter, in the circle of his family's arms.

The End

Dear Reader,

Thank you for reading *Winter's Wallflower*! I hope this eighth book in my *The Wicked Winters* series hit you right in the feelings and that Adele and Dom's happily ever after made you as happy to read as it made me to write. Thank you for spending your precious time reading my books!

Please consider leaving an honest review of *Winter's Wallflower*. Reviews are greatly appreciated! If you'd like to keep up to date with my latest releases and series news, sign up for my newsletter here or follow me on Amazon or BookBub. Join my reader's group on Facebook for bonus content, early excerpts, giveaways, and more.

But wait! There are more Winters on the way. Have we seen the last of Davy the pickpocket? Who was behind the attacks at The Devil's Spawn if it wasn't the Suttons? And what happens when Devil Winter has to play bodyguard for a fancy duke's daughter he can't seem to resist? If you'd like a preview of *Winter's Woman*, Book Nine in *The Wicked Winters* series, featuring the plucky Lady Evie Saltisford and the surly yet sexy Devil Winter, do read on.

Until next time,

Scarlett

Author's Note on Historical Accuracy

The Sutton Waterworks was inspired by similar water companies that were formed in East London in the early nineteenth century, particularly during the period of 1805-1810. Improved technology made water companies a booming investment opportunity for many businessmen, including, unfortunately, the unscrupulous.

My inspiration for Dominic Winter came in part from Joseph Merceron, who was something of a Regency-era gangster, wielding his power and corruption over a large portion of East End London during the same time period my *The Wicked Winters* series takes place.

According to eighteenth century records, tattooing was already a common practice in England prior to Captain Cook's famed encounter with tattooed Tahitians in 1769. Nineteenth century records, both written and then photographic as the century wore on, reveal a vast history of unique tattoos in all classes, including aristocrats.

I'm also deeply indebted to some excellent primary resources on carriages, fashion, and furniture of the Regency era. (Yes, Venetian blinds were in use, in case you wondered!) I sourced all the fun cant phrases Dom and his fellow bastard Winters use from *Memoirs of James Hardy Vaux*, printed in 1819. Now, do read on for that sneak peek I promised!

Winter's Woman
The Wicked Winters Book Nine
By
Scarlett Scott

The reigning toast of the Season, Lady Evangeline Saltisford is betrothed to the most eligible bachelor in London and a scant few weeks from having everything she has ever wanted. Until danger comes calling, and she is forced to accept aid from a decidedly unlikely—and infuriating—source.

Devil Winter is the illegitimate offspring of a wealthy merchant and a prostitute. He detests fancy aristocrats and has no patience for a cosseted duke's daughter. But he will do anything for his family, and when his older brother asks Devil to play bodyguard to Lady Evie, he has no choice but to accept the loathsome task.

Evie wants nothing to do with the boorish man from the rookeries who favors growls and glowers to polite manners. She is perfectly happy with her handsome, aristocratic fiancé. At least, that is what she tells herself. Until her gruff protector reveals a side she never imagined existed. A side she finds increasingly difficult to resist.

Devil is determined to eliminate the threat to Evie and cull her from his life. But being forced to remain by her side proves not so loathsome a duty. And before long, protecting the stunningly gorgeous duke's daughter is only the beginning of what Devil wants to do…

Chapter One

✻

London 1814

HER TWIN SISTER'S mind had turned to pudding.

That was the only reasonable explanation for the words that had just emerged from Lady Adele Winter's mouth.

Lady Evangeline Saltisford stared at her sister, doing her utmost to ignore the hulking monster lurking in the corner of the drawing room.

"You cannot be serious, Addy." Her eyes flicked to the glowering giant.

He was seated in a chair that was two sizes too small for him, and he looked ridiculous, surrounded by sleekly polished mahogany and all that gilt and silk. His eyes were a piercing shade of blue. Quite like the summer sky. Her stomach did a queer little flip as their gazes met and held. His bold lips tightened to a disapproving slash. She jerked her attention back to her sister, heat rising in her cheeks.

Addy shook her head, her expression mournful. "I am afraid this is no joking matter, Evie. Someone took a shot at you and Lord Denton while you were driving in the park."

"The shot in question likely emerged from a pair of drunkards engaged in a duel," Evie dismissed. "It had nothing to do with me."

The beast in the corner of the chamber grumbled something beneath his breath.

Evie cast another glance in his direction. There was something riveting about his face, and she did not like it. More heat curled through her. Her reaction to him was most odd. He could not be more different from her handsome betrothed, Lord Denton, who was golden-haired and slim, with patrician features and elegant hands.

Likely, it was the novelty of such a man. Like Addy's husband Mr. Dominic Winter, the man glaring at her hailed from the rookeries of the East End. Devil Winter was tall, broad, and feral-looking, with dark hair worn too long and massive fists, his handsome features set in a perpetual scowl. Everything about him screamed impropriety and the illicit.

And bedchamber romps.

What? No!

She was aghast at herself. Where had that errant thought emerged from? Hastily, she dashed it away.

"Devil is right," Addy was saying, snatching Evie's attention back once more. "We cannot be sure you were not the intended target. Until we know more, you will be safer with him watching over you."

Evie raised a brow. "He said all that? Odd. I could have sworn I heard nothing more than a growl."

The beast grunted.

She ignored him, tamping down the unsettled sensation trying to rise within her. Most unwanted. Unnecessary as well. She was happy with Lord Denton. Soon, she would be his wife. He was everything she had ever wanted in a husband. All she had to do was persuade her well-intentioned sister that having an ill-tempered man torn from the rookeries hanging about would be disastrous for Evie's impeccable reputation.

"Do be nice, Evie," Addy cautioned, frowning at her. "Devil is being quite generous, agreeing to keep you safe."

"Father will have an apoplectic fit when he discovers what you intend to do," she warned her sister in turn.

Their father, the Duke of Linross, had been called away from London to one of his country estates. With their mother still in Cornwall and their sister Hannah approaching her lying in, Evie had unceremoniously found herself being chaperoned by her twin sister, who was married to one of London's greatest rogues. The potential scandal was bad enough, but her sister's suggestion a hulking beast who went by the name *Devil* ought to offer her protection… Why, it was ludicrous.

"Our father will be grateful I have taken the threat to you seriously and done my sisterly duty." Addy smiled.

"Lord Denton will not like it," she tried next, knowing her betrothed would disapprove most heartily.

Denton adhered to propriety above all else. He had not even attempted to kiss her yet, much to Evie's dismay.

A low growl emanated from the corner of the drawing room, followed by a deep, booming baritone. "Then Denton can go fu—"

"Yes, you are right, Devil," Addy interrupted brightly. "Lord Denton need not know. When you are here at home, Devil will never be far from your side. When you are in public, he will follow you discreetly. Is that not right, Devil?"

He grunted once more.

"No," Evie said mulishly. "I do not *want* him at my side. Nor do I require protection."

"It is necessary, Evie, for your wellbeing." Addy was stern. Insistent.

Evie frowned. "He is menacing, Addy." She lowered her voice to a whisper. "I do not like him."

"Heard that," he growled. "Feeling's mutual."

Evie's gaze returned to him. Their stares clashed, the

connection sending a visceral jolt through her. She could not seem to look away. The certain knowledge that Devil Winter was going to cause her a great deal of trouble lodged in her heart like a thorn.

Want more? Get *Winter's Woman*!

Don't miss Scarlett's other romances!
(Listed by Series)

Complete Book List
scarlettscottauthor.com/books

HISTORICAL ROMANCE

Heart's Temptation
A Mad Passion (Book One)
Rebel Love (Book Two)
Reckless Need (Book Three)
Sweet Scandal (Book Four)
Restless Rake (Book Five)
Darling Duke (Book Six)
The Night Before Scandal (Book Seven)

Wicked Husbands
Her Errant Earl (Book One)
Her Lovestruck Lord (Book Two)
Her Reformed Rake (Book Three)
Her Deceptive Duke (Book Four)
Her Missing Marquess (Book Five)
Her Virtuous Viscount (Book Six)

League of Dukes
Nobody's Duke (Book One)
Heartless Duke (Book Two)
Dangerous Duke (Book Three)
Shameless Duke (Book Four)
Scandalous Duke (Book Five)
Fearless Duke (Book Six)

Notorious Ladies of London
Lady Ruthless (Book One)
Lady Wallflower (Book Two)
Lady Reckless (Book Three)
Lady Wicked (Book Four)

The Wicked Winters
Wicked in Winter (Book One)
Wedded in Winter (Book Two)
Wanton in Winter (Book Three)
Wishes in Winter (Book 3.5)
Willful in Winter (Book Four)
Wagered in Winter (Book Five)
Wild in Winter (Book Six)
Wooed in Winter (Book Seven)
Winter's Wallflower (Book Eight)
Winter's Woman (Book Nine)
Winter's Whispers (Book Ten)

Stand-alone Novella
Lord of Pirates

CONTEMPORARY ROMANCE

Love's Second Chance
Reprieve (Book One)
Perfect Persuasion (Book Two)
Win My Love (Book Three)

Coastal Heat
Loved Up (Book One)

About the Author

USA Today and Amazon bestselling author Scarlett Scott writes steamy Victorian and Regency romance with strong, intelligent heroines and sexy alpha heroes. She lives in Pennsylvania with her Canadian husband, adorable identical twins, and one TV-loving dog.

A self-professed literary junkie and nerd, she loves reading anything, but especially romance novels, poetry, and Middle English verse. Catch up with her on her website www.scarlettscottauthor.com. Hearing from readers never fails to make her day.

Scarlett's complete book list and information about upcoming releases can be found at www.scarlettscottauthor.com.

Connect with Scarlett! You can find her here:
Join Scarlett Scott's reader's group on Facebook for early excerpts, giveaways, and a whole lot of fun!
Sign up for her newsletter here.
scarlettscottauthor.com/contact
Follow Scarlett on Amazon
Follow Scarlett on BookBub
www.instagram.com/scarlettscottauthor
www.twitter.com/scarscoromance
www.pinterest.com/scarlettscott
www.facebook.com/AuthorScarlettScott
Join the Historical Harlots on Facebook

Printed in Dunstable, United Kingdom